HER
MOTHERHOOD
WISH

BY
ANNE FRASER

MILLS & BOON

For Kim, one of life's special people. Thanks for listening and thanks for making me laugh. You'll be sorely missed.

First published in Great Britain 2012
by Mills & Boon, an imprint of Harlequin (UK) Limited.
Harlequin (UK) Limited, Eton House, 18-24 Paradise Road, Richmond, Surrey TW9 1SR

© Anne Fraser 2012

ISBN: 978 0 263 22887 8

ROM

Harlequin (UK) policy is to use papers that are natural, renewable and recyclable products and made from wood grown in sustainable forests. The logging and manufacturing process conform to the legal environmental regulations of the country of origin.

Printed and bound in Great Britain
by CPI Antony Rowe, Chippenham, Wiltshire

Anne Fraser was born in Scotland, but brought up in South Africa. After she left school she returned to the birthplace of her parents, the remote Western Islands of Scotland. She left there to train as a nurse, before going on to university to study English Literature. After the birth of her first child she and her doctor husband travelled the world, working in rural Africa, Australia and Northern Canada. Anne still works in the health sector. To relax, she enjoys spending time with her family, reading, walking and travelling.

Recent titles by the same author:

THE FIREBRAND WHO UNLOCKED HIS HEART
MISTLETOE, MIDWIFE…MIRACLE BABY
DOCTOR ON THE RED CARPET
THE PLAYBOY OF HARLEY STREET
THE DOCTOR AND THE DEBUTANTE
DAREDEVIL, DOCTOR…DAD!†
MIRACLE: MARRIAGE REUNITED
SPANISH DOCTOR, PREGNANT MIDWIFE*

*_The Brides of Penhally Bay_
†_St Piran's Hospital_

These books are also available in eBook format from www.millsandboon.co.uk

CHAPTER ONE

My darling Josh,

I am writing this to you, knowing it may be years before you read it. If you are reading this, it means I have lost you.

And if I lost you you're probably not even called Josh now. But whatever name your father has chosen to give you, I hope you have had a wonderful life so far. I know your father loves you, otherwise he wouldn't have fought so hard to keep you.

I love you too. More than I can say. I loved you before you were even growing inside me and as you grew I loved you more. I still love you—I hope you have never doubted that.

I wonder what kind of man you turned out to be. I wonder what your childhood was like. It tears me apart thinking of you growing up without me. I almost can't bear to imagine it and I want you to know that I tried to do everything in my power to keep you.

I enclose the newspaper cuttings from the time I was pregnant with you. It may help you understand what happened and why I had to give you up.

You will always be in my prayers. If you ever want to find me, I'll be waiting. If you don't, I'll

understand that too. All I want, my darling child,
is for you to be happy.
Your birth mother,
Olivia Simpson

Four months earlier

DAVID leaned against the pillar, nursing his coffee and
making the most of the last few minutes he had before he
was due in Theatre. The early morning sun warmed his
skin, promising another glorious day in San Francisco.

Shortly he'd be putting in a shunt for a patient with
hydrocephalus. He'd done several like it before and all
the patients had recovered well. He hoped, however,
that the theatre staff here would be as good as the ones
in his last hospital in New York. Theatre staff became
teams, knowing instinctively after a while what the surgeon needed and when. No doubt it would take time before he and his new team meshed, and in the meantime
he—and they—would have to be patient.

He watched idly as a Volkswagen Beetle pulled into
the car park with its roof down.

The woman at the wheel immediately caught his attention. In a city of beautiful women she was still stun-
ning. She had thick blonde hair that was held back from
her face with a scarf. Her eyes were hidden by oversized
sunglasses, but her full, wide mouth was turned up at
the corners as if she were enjoying some private joke.

The car came to a stop a few yards away from where
he was standing and as he swallowed the last of his coffee, the driver's door opened and he caught a glimpse
of slim, tanned legs peeking out from a yellow sun-
dress. As the woman reached over to pick something

up from the passenger seat, her dress inched tantalisingly up her thigh.

She pushed her car door open further with her foot and eased her way out of the car, clutching a heavy armload of files to her chest as she did so.

The yellow dress and her blonde hair made him think bizarrely of a sunbeam. He should really go and help her, but he was enjoying himself too much.

She kicked the car door closed, and as she did so, the files slid to the ground, where they fanned out in an untidy heap. As she swore under her breath, David threw his paper coffee cup in the bin and pushed himself away from the wall.

She was crouching by the files, her canary-yellow dress once more riding up to reveal the best legs David had seen in a while.

'Need some help, ma'am?' he drawled, and without waiting for a reply hunkered down beside her and reached for the papers.

'Thank you. If you wouldn't mind,' she said in an English accent. She lifted her sunglasses and pushed them on top of her head. Bright green eyes caught his for a second and something shifted behind his ribs. She might have the best pair of pins he'd seen in a while, but those eyes. Man, a guy could lose himself there for a while. The rest of her wasn't too bad either. Her nose was pert, a little too turned up for some tastes perhaps, but he thought it made her look cute. Without that nose her face would have been too perfect, too severe almost. He'd dated enough perfect-looking women and after a while they began to merge into one. The way this woman looked…well, she wasn't so easily forgettable.

He reached for a book that had slithered under her car. He read the title as he passed it to her. Mmm…interesting reading. Not just beautiful, but bright. Unless of course the book was for someone else. That was okay too. Brains were a plus, but not essential.

Instinctively he glanced at her hands. No ring. That was good. He had a date for tonight, but he could easily cancel. Plead pressure of work or something. Now he needed a name and a number to add to his growing collection.

'I'm Dr Stuart,' he said easily. 'One of the neurosurgeons.' That, he found, never failed to impress.

Didn't seem to be working with this one, however. She raised an eyebrow, looking amused.

'Indeed?' She smiled showing even white teeth. 'I would offer to shake your hand but…' she indicated the files in her arms '…I don't fancy having to pick them all up again.'

He, on the other hand, would be quite happy to spend another few minutes looking into those green eyes. Later. There would definitely be later. Would she be a dinner-and-a-show girl, or an outdoorsy one? He was looking forward to finding out.

He placed a hand under her elbow to help her up to her feet.

He was checking out the rest of her and just about to move on to stage two when he noticed something that sent a wave of regret from his libido to his brain. She was pregnant. No doubt about it. The way her yellow dress clung to her slim frame emphasised the swell of her belly. Around sixteen weeks, he guessed. And just when it was going so well.

Her eyes held his and the corners creased with amusement as she seemed to notice his reaction.

'Thank you, Dr Stuart.' Her smile was wide and mischievous.

'You're welcome.' Damn. His timing was off on this one. His mind shifted away. There was no reason to cancel Melissa after all, and if her dark hair and liquid eyes seemed less appealing now, it was only because this buttercup-yellow woman had made him think of sunshine rather than a cool winter evening.

His pager bleeped insistently. That would be the theatre nurse letting him know that his patient was on his way. His thoughts moved away from the buttercup woman and towards the theatre. Images of the structures of the brain were forming in his head, as they always did just before he operated. He had approximately ten minutes to get changed and into Theatre.

He smiled in the direction of buttercup woman.

'Got to go and save a life. See you around,' he said, and spun on his heel. Two seconds later he'd forgotten all about her.

Olivia pushed her way through the double doors and into the emergency room, still grinning. What an idiot Dr Stuart was. Did he honestly use that line? *I'm a neurosurgeon and I save lives!* Good grief. And did women actually fall for it? Admittedly, he was gorgeous, with his wide, sexy smile and platinum eyes. His physique wasn't too bad either. Even under his scrubs she could discern the lines of his muscular legs and broad shoulders. Clearly he was a man who worked out.

As usual, ER was already going like a fair. Most of the chairs in the waiting room were occupied. Two gurneys were lined up in the corridor, with patients waiting to be taken to the wards, and in one of the exam rooms she saw several shadowed figures through the semi-opaque glass as her colleagues from the night shift worked over a patient.

Kelly, the chief ER nurse, barely glanced at her as Olivia placed the folders down on the reception desk.

'Morning, Livvy,' Kelly said, without lifting her head. 'Welcome to another day in hell.'

Olivia knew Kelly didn't mean it. The ER nurse had worked in the department for years, and despite her claims that she would sail off into the sunset in a heartbeat if only she would win the lottery, everyone knew she was lying through her teeth. The department without Kelly was as unthinkable as Kelly without the department. The staff often joked that Kelly must live in the hospital as she always seemed to be there when they arrived, and was there again when they came back the next morning.

'What do we have?'

This time Kelly did raise her head. 'The usual mix— three suspected fractures, one MI, half a dozen with vague symptoms that have to be investigated, and an elderly lady they're working on in exam room one.' She pushed a carton of sugary doughnuts towards Olivia. 'Help yourself. You're going to need at least five to get through the day.'

Olivia glanced longingly at the carton. Doughnuts were her favourite. At one time she had survived on them, washing them down with strong black coffee. But these days she feasted on fruit and oats and refused to let anything without a vitamin past her lips.

She shook her head and regretfully pushed the box back across the counter well away from temptation. 'No, thanks. Proper food is all I'm eating these days.'

'And how is that working out for you?' Kelly said, with a sarcastic lift of her eyebrow. 'You disappoint me, Dr Simpson. I thought I had found an ally in this city where no one eats real food, and now I find you have gone over to the other side!' She smiled. 'I have to say, for someone who eats nothing but rabbit food, you are looking good, girl. And how is that baby doing?'

Kelly was one of the few people who knew the whole story behind Olivia's pregnancy. The others speculated, Olivia knew, and that was hardly surprising. Since Richard had died, she hadn't dated anyone, to their knowledge. Yet here she was, pregnant. Their curiosity was natural, but that didn't mean she was prepared to go into long, elaborate explanations. Her pregnancy was her business.

She patted her stomach protectively. She had waited a long time for this baby. All she wanted to do was enjoy every moment of being pregnant. She only wished Richard was still alive to enjoy it with her.

Her heart still ached when she thought of Richard, but somewhere over the last couple of years the intense, breath-robbing pain had eased. It had been three years since he'd died and slowly she'd come to accept that it was time to start a new chapter in her life. She'd promised Richard, after all.

Unexpectedly, an image of the man she'd met in the car park flashed into her head. Despite his bad taste in chat-up lines, he really was a hunk—if you liked that sort of casual look. He'd been unshaven—not totally professional for a surgeon—but she only had to think of his grin and her heart turned over.

She pushed the image away. Men were still off the agenda. Typical, though. The first time she had found a man that had made her pulse bounce, he was an idiot. Not that what she thought made the slightest difference, given her condition. Nevertheless, she was curious.

'I met someone in the car park,' she said casually as Kelly shoved a herbal tea in her direction. 'Dr Stuart, I think he said his name was. I haven't seen him about. Is he new?'

Kelly eyed her with amused exasperation. 'Not you too! What planet have you been on? The nurses and female doctors have been talking about nothing else lately. Dr Stuart has joined us from New York. Started last week.' Kelly always knew everything about the hospital. She made it her business to know. 'He was in this morning when we admitted a patient with a head injury. I'd almost swear the nurses arranged it so they could get him down here for a consult!' Kelly's eyes were twinkling as she lifted an eyebrow. 'Don't tell me he's managed to capture the cool Dr Simpson's attention? That would be a first.'

Olivia moved across to the board keeping her back towards Kelly so she wouldn't see that her face was hot. 'Don't be silly, Kelly. I'm hardly in the market for a man.'

'Just as well,' Kelly replied. 'In the short time he's been at the hospital he's taken two of the staff out on dates. The man is a mass of walking pheromones. Let's hope he's as good a surgeon as he is at making pulses rise.'

Olivia felt curiously disappointed. So the way he'd looked at her, as if she were the only woman in the world, *was* all an act. But why should it matter? As she'd told Kelly, she wasn't looking for a relationship. She had more than enough to be getting on with.

The phone that linked them to the emergency services rang and Olivia's attention focussed on Kelly.

'We'll expect you,' Kelly said, replacing the phone after listening for a few moments. She stood and immediately was all business. 'Male. Forty. Suspected stroke. ETA ten minutes. Let's get to work.'

* * *

Although Brad Schwimmer was displaying the signs of someone who had some sort of cerebral event, Olivia wasn't sure what it was. His speech was unintelligible and he was disoriented, but Olivia didn't believe he'd had a stroke.

His wife, a distraught woman in her early thirties called Sally, watched anxiously as the nurses cut away her husband's clothes and attached him to the monitors.

'I did the school run. I was away longer than usual—for over an hour. I met a friend I hadn't seen for a while and we chatted. When I got back I thought he'd gone to work, but then I went into the kitchen and he was just lying there.'

'BP one hundred and two over fifty-six, pulse rapid and weak,' one of the nurses called out.

'How was he this morning?' Olivia asked. 'Was he complaining of anything? A headache? Feeling dizzy? Sick?'

'No, he'd just come back from his run before I left. He goes every morning before work—when he's at home, that is.'

'Does he travel much?'

'He's a sales executive. He travels out of the country for a few days most weeks. Is he going to be all right? Please! You have to help him!'

'We'll do everything we can, I promise. But first we're going to have to do a few tests to find out what exactly we're dealing with. Would you like to wait in the family room?'

'I want to stay with him. Please let me. I promise I won't get in your way.'

'Okay, Sally. He'll probably find it reassuring to have you here. Talk to him. It's possible that he can still hear what we're saying even though he's not responding. When was he last away?'

'He just came back from Thailand yesterday.'

Thailand. Recent foreign travel added a long list of possible diagnoses they had to rule out. Although rare, Japanese encephalitis was one possibility.

'Was he vaccinated for encephalitis? And did he take prophylaxis for malaria before he left?' she asked. Cerebral malaria was something else she should exclude.

'He always takes the meds he's supposed to. He knows the risks if he doesn't. He's very particular about his health.'

'Could we get a consult from Infectious Diseases?' Olivia asked. Something wasn't adding up. 'In the meantime, let's get a CT scan of his head and draw blood for a full infection screen, including malaria. Keep him on twenty-eight per cent oxygen.'

'Dr Simpson?' One of the interns popped her head through the door. 'Dr Scutari is asking for help in room two if you're free?'

Olivia peeled off her gloves and apron and chucked them in the bin. 'I'm on my way.' She turned to the nurses. 'I'll be next door. Call me if there is any change, or when the attending from Infectious Diseases gets here.'

This was typical of the ER on a weekday morning. Often it was busy and there was no predicting what they'd get in. It was what she loved about working here. Not everyone enjoyed the high-octane atmosphere, but most of them who worked in the department loved the buzz.

She helped the intern deal with his patient, a straight-forward MI, then returned to Resus and was surprised to find Dr Stuart bending over her patient. However, if she was surprised to see him, he looked floored to see her.

'You're a doctor! Why didn't you say?' he said, glancing up at her.

Because you didn't give me the chance. Because once you saw I was pregnant, I might as well have been invisible. Of course none of that could be said out loud but it didn't mean she wasn't enjoying his discomfort. That would teach him to go around introducing himself as a neurosurgeon to strange women.

'I'm Dr Olivia Simpson. ER resident.' She smiled briefly in his direction. In the time she'd been away, dealing with the other patient, Brad had lost some of his pallor. However, there was no improvement in his conscious level. 'I didn't ask for a neuro consult.' She raised her voice. 'Do we have Brad's CT scan?'

'I have it here.' Candice, one of the ER nurses, flicked on a screen.

'Besides, aren't you supposed to be in Theatre—saving lives?' Olivia couldn't resist adding, *sotto voce*, as he stepped alongside her to study the scan.

He didn't even look mildly embarrassed. 'I was. Job done. I was at a loose end so I thought I'd come down to the ER to see if you had anything for me. Failing that, I hoped to scrounge a cup of coffee.'

Job done? She couldn't have been in the department more than twenty minutes before her patient had arrived. Take another twenty-five when she'd been examining Brad and helping Dr Scutari—he was still done pretty quickly. What sort of neurological procedure took so little time? She hoped to hell Dr Stuart knew what he was doing.

'Now you're here, what do you think?' She gestured to the screen.

'I'm pretty sure he has an infarct of the right cere-
bellum,' he said after only a few moments. He pointed
to the area of the brain he was talking about. 'But we
need to find out what caused it. I'm guessing a clot. We
should let the radiologists do an angiogram. If there is
a clot they can be pretty good at aspirating it.'

Dr Stuart turned to Sally, who had been listening to
the exchange with frightened, uncomprehending eyes.

'We think that your husband might have a blood clot
blocking an artery inside his brain. That's what is making him so unresponsive. There is a procedure that can
help. The radiologists put a catheter, a fine tube, into the
artery in his groin and locate the blockage. If there is a
clot present, they'll try to suck it out.'

'But…' Olivia shot Dr Stuart a warning look '…you
should be aware that the procedure carries some risks.'

'What kind of risks?' Sally's voice rose to a squeak.

'It's possible that the procedure could well make
whatever is wrong with your husband worse.'

'On the other hand, if he doesn't have it, he may not
improve from where he is.' Dr Stuart interrupted.

Typical of a surgeon, Olivia seethed. Any chance to
intervene and they always took it over the more con-
servative approaches. She kept her voice level and matter-of-fact. 'If Brad has had a stroke then he might well
improve over the coming months.'

'That's true,' David said easily. 'But until we do the
angiogram we won't know for certain. Here's what I
suggest we do. We get him up to the MRI suite, ask the
radiologists to take a look, and make a decision from
there. How does that sound, Dr Simpson?'

It was, Olivia had to admit, a sensible approach. There
was no point at this stage in giving the wife options and

possibly scaring her further until they knew what the radiologists had to say.

'Why don't you come up and, if my diagnosis proves correct, watch the procedure?' Dr Stuart said to Olivia. 'You'll find it interesting. The radiologists can do some pretty amazing stuff.'

'Let me check what Kelly has waiting first, but if they can spare me, yes, I'd like to watch.'

Olivia took Sally by the hand and spoke soothingly to her. 'Try not to worry too much until we hear what the radiologists have to say. Then we can decide how to proceed from there.'

Candice looked across at them. She was positively preening under the neurosurgeon's gaze. 'I'll check that they're free upstairs, shall I?'

David flashed her a grin and Candice blushed to the roots of her hair. 'That would be helpful,' he said.

Sally looked relieved that she didn't have to make a decision just yet. Olivia gave her shoulder one final squeeze and went in search of Kelly. She had only got a few steps when she heard Dr Stuart's voice coming from behind her.

'Good thing I was in the department.'

She whirled around. 'I'd have seen it eventually, Dr Stuart.'

'It's David.' He cocked his head to the side and regarded her from his silvery eyes. 'But you might have wasted time getting the Infectious Disease consult. You can cancel them.'

'Shouldn't we wait?'

'Absolutely not. I'm almost certain. Brad needs the blockage cleared—either an angioplasty or clot aspiration—and the sooner the better. I'm the attending, so the decision is mine.'

Olivia's pulse was racing and she wasn't sure why. Perhaps it had something to do with the way his grey-blue eyes locked onto hers. She shook her head slightly in an attempt to regain her focus. He was right. This was his area of expertise. She was letting her peculiar reaction to him make her flustered, behave out of character and question his judgement.

'I'm happy to wait to see what the radiologists have to say,' David continued mildly, 'but I'm convinced they'll confirm my diagnosis. We can discuss it before speaking to his wife about his treatment options. Okay?'

Olivia forced a smile. 'Fine by me.'

She turned to the head ER nurse, who had been watching the exchange with obvious amusement. 'Kelly, is there anything you need me for in the next hour or so?'

'If there is, I'll page you. There are other doctors on duty, you know.' It was a barbed reference to the fact that Olivia liked to be involved in as many cases as she could. Apart from Kelly, Olivia was often first in and last out. As chief resident, the work of the interns was her overall responsibility—a responsibility she took very seriously indeed. Just because she was going on maternity leave in a few months was no reason to let her standards slip.

David reached across Olivia and swooped down on the box of doughnuts. 'Worth coming down here just for this,' he said as he took a bite out of one.

Olivia glanced at her watch. 'We don't have time.' She reached across and removed the remains of the doughnut from his hand and chucked it in the bin. David stared. He lifted an eyebrow and grinned.

Kelly looked at Olivia and then at David. 'You're causing a bit of a ruckus in my department, young man. I just hope you're as good a surgeon as everyone says you are.'

* * *

Upstairs in Radiology, Olivia watched as they injected dye through the arterial catheter in Brad's groin. David murmured something to the radiologist when almost immediately a blocked vessel showed up on the screen. 'There's our culprit. The vessel wall looks quite normal so it must be blocked by a fresh blood clot,' David said. He turned to Olivia. 'There's no time to talk to his wife—we have to remove it.'

The radiologist inserted a suction adapter onto the groin catheter and Olivia held her breath as he carefully sucked out the clot. Within minutes Brad's eyes opened briefly to the call of his name and he appeared to look at them purposefully.

David lifted his head and grinned at her. 'Pretty impressive, huh?'

Olivia nodded. It was a procedure she hadn't witnessed before. And as David had said, it was pretty dramatic.

'I'll let his wife know he's regained consciousness,' she said.

She left the X-ray suite and hurried back downstairs, Kelly's words echoing in her mind. David might be as good a surgeon as everyone said he was. Pity about the rest.

Olivia tossed her car keys onto the table by the door before going into the kitchen and pouring herself a glass of water. The remainder of her shift in the ER had been hectic. Not long after she'd come back down from Radiology a multiple RTA had come in. It had been an hour after her shift was due to finish when they'd finally sorted everyone out and either sent them home or to the OR. Thankfully all the casualties had survived.

She tipped some dog food into Bouncer's bowl, which

he devoured in three quick mouthfuls. When he looked up at her hopefully she shook her head.

'No, you know you'll get fat, Bouncer. I'm doing this for your own good. I'll take you for a walk in a moment.' Bouncer, her three-year-old Labrador, attended doggy day care whenever Olivia was on duty. It meant a detour on the way to and from the hospital, but he was worth it. She shouldn't really have a dog at all, she knew that, not with the hours she worked, but he was company for her and taking him for long walks kept her fit.

Taking her water through to the sitting room, she eased off her shoes and rubbed her aching feet. Bouncer plonked himself next to her and laid his head on her knee, nudging her arm with his wet nose.

'Okay, bossy boots, I get the message. You want your head scratched.' Rubbing Bouncer's golden fur, she clicked on the TV remote. Not that she really wanted to watch the news or follow some trashy reality show, it was more to fill the house with noise. When she and Richard had first viewed the house in Sea Cliff, they'd both known instantly it was the perfect forever home for them. It had spectacular views of the Golden Gate Bridge and the Pacific, and with its six bedrooms and three reception rooms had been more than large enough to entertain Richard's business colleagues and clients. Most importantly, though, it was spacious enough to be filled with the children they had both longed to have together.

Now, without him in it, it just felt big and cold and empty. She'd considered selling it several times since Richard had died, but at first she hadn't wanted to leave the house that still smelled of him, still held his memory in every room—especially the uncompleted nursery. Then, when the shadow of grief had lifted and she'd returned to work, she'd simply been too busy. Perhaps now was the right time to find a new home for her and the baby? Somewhere cosy with a smaller, more manageable garden and a playroom? Of course she would always miss Richard, and she would have his baby to remember him by, but the life they had shared was in the past. Hadn't she promised herself a new start? Wasn't having this baby the beginning of that? But with work and her pregnancy it was unlikely she'd get around to finding somewhere else to live now.

It wasn't as if money was a problem. Richard had left her so well off that she'd never have to work again if she didn't want to. But she did want to work. It was what kept her sane. She'd have to stop, of course, for a while at least, when this baby came along, but eventually she'd go back. Being single, she'd have to employ a nanny but, assuming she found the right person, that would be okay. She'd already asked an agency to start looking.

She placed a hand over her swelling stomach. 'Not too long now, baby,' she whispered. She should be relishing this brief interlude of peace and quiet, because when the baby came there wouldn't be much of it. Not that she didn't yearn to hold her child. Even another twenty-two weeks seemed an eternity.

She rested her head on the back of the couch and unexpectedly an image of David filled her mind. What was it about him that made her react the way she did? She'd never been attracted to his type before. The type that thought all he had to do was smile and a woman would melt.

She grimaced. To be honest, she had melted. Just a little bit. She'd liked the frank and blatant approval in his eyes. It had made her tingle, and that had made her feel good. More than good—it had made her feel alive. What woman wouldn't feel flattered being admired by such a devastatingly attractive man? Until he'd seen her bump, of course. Then she had disappeared so far off his radar she might as well have been in outer space. Olivia tutted. Dr David Stuart might be gorgeous but he wasn't for her. Especially now. All her love, affection and attention were going to be devoted to the child growing inside her—Richard's child and hers. All things considered, David would have to remain where he belonged. In the realms of fantasy.

Bouncer was snoring contentedly so Olivia eased herself off the couch, careful not to disturb him. She crossed over to the French doors and stepped out onto the balcony. The lights of the Golden Gate Bridge twinkled in the night sky and a gentle breeze carried the sounds of distant traffic. Strange how this view always seemed to soothe her and fill her with renewed energy and hope. Perhaps it was the reminder that life went on, no matter how much you wanted time to stand still. *And, oh, my God, Richard, I wanted time to stop before you died.* But it hadn't and she'd had to come to terms with life without him. She wrapped her arms around herself. In a few months she would have their baby and at least a part of Richard would live on.

CHAPTER TWO

OLIVIA bent over her patient in Resus as the nurses cut away his shirt and trousers. The accompanying paramedic recited the known facts about the casualty.

According to witnesses, a truck had made a right turn and his wing mirror had knocked the cyclist from his bike. The lorry driver was shocked but unharmed. When it came to a battle between a ten-ton truck and a push bike there was only ever one winner.

The cyclist was already wired to the monitors. His pulse was slow and his breathing shallow. She opened an eyelid and shone her torch. The pupil of the left eye did as it was supposed to, but the other was blown.

Very gently she removed his helmet, noting the blood stains on the back. Quickly she palpated along the skull until she found what she was looking for—a depression a couple of inches above the neck. Unconscious, skull fracture, unequal pupils—it all added up. He must have a haematoma causing compression of the brain stem.

'I need a consult from Neuro,' she said briskly. But, as always, the nurse had anticipated her order and was already on the phone.

'They're just finishing in Theatre. Someone will be here as soon as they can.'

'Tell them I need them here, stat,' Olivia said. Her

patient had to have the pressure in his head relieved, and as soon as possible. With every second that passed his brain was swelling, pushing against the rigid bones of the skull.

'I've found some ID,' one of the nurses called out. 'Your patient's name is Mark Lightbody. He's thirty-three. There's also a number for his wife. I'll give her a call and tell her to come.'

Olivia nodded. Poor Mrs Lightbody was about to have her day—possibly her life—ruined.

Mark was unconscious, and although he was still breathing unaided, she had to intubate him to secure his airway and maintain his oxygen levels. The measures she'd taken would keep him stable for a while, but surgery was the only way to relieve the growing pressure on his brain. She glanced at the clock on the wall. Five minutes had passed since Kelly had phoned. Where the hell was the neurosurgeon?

Just when she was about to insist that Kelly phone again, the swing doors burst open and Dr Stuart strode in. She'd only seen him in passing since that first day and she was dismayed to note that her already escalated pulse upped another notch.

'What do you have for me?' he asked her as Candice stepped forward with a disposable gown.

'Mark Lightbody. Cyclist with an occipital skull fracture. GCS six. Right pupil fixed and dilated. Left pupil responding normally. Apart from the injury to his head, he has only minor cuts and lacerations. He needs emergency surgery to relieve the pressure on his brain.'

David grinned. 'Doesn't the attending—as in me—usually make that decision?'

As he was talking he was examining Mark. 'But I have to agree. Unfortunately the theatre is still being scrubbed after our last case. It will take at least ten minutes to get another ready. He needs a craniotomy, so we'll have to do it here.'

'Here?' Olivia echoed.

'No reason why not. I assume you have a tray set up for that purpose?'

'Yes, but shouldn't we wait to get him to the OR?'

'It will take time to get him to the OR. Time he doesn't have—not unless we want to risk him dying or ending up severely brain damaged. In my opinion, doing a craniotomy here and now is his best chance. Now, we can waste more time by arguing, in which case I suggest you step out and attend to other patients, or we can get on with the procedure.'

Olivia felt the blood rush to her cheeks. She hadn't been objecting to carrying out the procedure, just querying whether it would be better to wait until they'd taken him to Theatre. However, every minute they wasted arguing was time Mark didn't have. She bit back the sharp retort that had risen to her lips and nodded. 'I'll stay and assist.'

The insufferable arrogance of the man. However, she wasn't about to rise to the bait.

'In fact,' he said, 'why don't you do it while I assist?'

Olivia felt a frisson of excitement. She always grabbed any opportunity to acquire additional skills. His confidence in her was flattering and his aura of self-confidence immensely reassuring. Not all the attendings were prepared to teach the ER residents. 'Thanks. I'd like to,' she replied.

She scrubbed while Kelly set up the tray and one of the other nurses shaved Mark's blood-matted hair and prepped the surgical field.

'Good. I'll show you how to get started then you can take over.'

David made a wide incision in the scalp below the dent in Mark's head and peeled back the skin to expose an obvious depressed fracture of the skull. 'This is the interesting bit. Take these elevators…' he handed her two '…and lift the bone fragments up out of the way.'

Everyone seemed to hold their breath as Olivia did as David asked.

As soon as she'd lifted the shattered bone out of the way, a fat red blood clot bulged out towards her. Slowly and very carefully she removed the clotted blood and a satisfied glow spread through her as Mark's vitals immediately improved.

She grinned at David. When he smiled back something seemed to tilt inside her chest, making her catch her breath. She dipped her head and concentrated on replacing the bone.

'Good job, Dr Simpson. I'll get him into the OR, patch up the skull fracture properly and repair the scalp incision.'

David peeled off his plastic apron and dropped it in the bin. The two ER nurses who were standing by exchanged smiles.

'Could we get him up to the OR pronto?' David asked. He removed his protective goggles and winked— winked!—at one of the nurses, who blushed furiously.

'Thank you, Doctor,' Olivia said stiffly. 'We'll get that organised.'

David indicated with a nod of his head that she accompany him outside. Olivia went with him, knowing if she didn't he was likely to have his say in front of the staff.

But to her amazement he didn't launch into an attack. 'I meant what I said back there. Good work,' he said. 'You have the steady, delicate touch of a surgeon.'

Instinctively Olivia looked down at her hands. Did he guess that at one time she'd thought of being a surgeon? But that had been before Richard had become ill. Then the long hours and years the training would have required had been out of the question. She'd never regretted the decision, and when Richard had gone into remission and they'd decided to grab the chance to have a family, her dream of becoming a surgeon had faded into second place. The hours she'd worked in the ER had been long and hard enough as it was.

'I wasn't trying to argue with you earlier,' she said quietly. 'I was only wondering whether it would be better for our patient to wait until we got him to ER.'

His grin grew wider. 'Hey, think nothing of it.' He winked again, then his smile vanished and he lowered his voice. 'Despite anything you might have heard about me, or will hear, I'm a bloody good surgeon. It is the one thing I take seriously. I expect we will brush up against each other in ER pretty often, so it is as well that you know.'

Brush up against each other! To her mortification an image of them brushing up against each other flashed into her mind. And it didn't have anything to do with being in the emergency room. The blood rushed to her cheeks. Good God, did every pregnant woman's brain turn to mush like this? Or was there something wrong with her?

'I don't intend to tussle with you every time we disagree about how to treat a patient,' David continued. 'Just as I won't argue with you when you make an ER decision.' He shot her a quizzical look but his eyes were glinting. 'Hey, is it warm in here or what?'

'They always keep the ER too warm,' she said as nonchalantly as she could.

Candice came out of Resus and hurried towards them.

'They say they'll be ready for you in the OR in ten minutes, Dr Stuart.'

Without warning, an image of Mark's exposed brain flashed back into Olivia's mind, but instead of Mark she saw Richard on the operating table. To her mortification, her eyes filled. This damn pregnancy was playing hell with her emotions.

David seemed to do a double take and the smile left his eyes. 'Damn. You're crying. Is it something I said?'

Even more mortified, Olivia tried a smile. She blinked the tears away and pointed to her face. 'Pregnancy hormones. Sorry. They've turned me into the oddest person—someone I don't recognise.'

A strange expression crossed David's face. Had she not known better she would have said it was regret, but just at that moment a white-faced woman carrying a toddler rushed through the doors and up to the reception desk. 'I'm Mrs Lightbody. I understand my husband, Mark, is here. Where is he? Is he all right?'

'Shall we have a word?' David asked, tilting his head in the woman's direction. 'Or I can do it alone, if you need a moment.'

Olivia grabbed a tissue from the box on the counter and blew her nose. Then she looked him in the eye. 'See! Back to a normal person. Told you it wouldn't last. Let's go and put Mark's wife out of her misery.'

That evening Olivia left the ER later than usual. She was tired, and the thought of going home to her empty home held little appeal. She groaned as she remembered that she hadn't been shopping for a while and ran a mental inventory of her fridge contents in her head. A couple of eggs, some stale bread and orange juice. That was it. Damn.

Although she wasn't hungry, she had to think about the baby. Not for the first time, she sent a silent prayer heavenwards when she thought of the deli a few streets away from where she lived. It had a few tables and served delicious home-cooked meals. She ate there at least once a week.

As she stepped out into the car park, she saw a familiar figure bent over a bicycle. David was studying a flat tyre and looking around as if he expected a replacement wheel to appear out of nowhere. She'd passed him once or twice on her way into work and he had always been on his bike. It had surprised her. If anything, she would have expected him to ride a Harley-Davidson or a sports car. Maybe he did it for effect? He probably knew that he looked pretty damn sexy in his sleeveless T-shirt and cycling shorts. God! Now she was getting all hot under the collar again.

For a moment she was tempted to walk past as if she hadn't seen him. She really was too tired to deal with someone as exhausting as David, but then good manners got the better of her. He'd helped her the other day, so she could hardly leave him to his own devices.

'Problem?' she asked. When he looked up her breath caught in her throat. He really was the most astonishingly good-looking man, despite the five-o'clock shadow that looked as if it were about to become a beard. Was he trying to grow one? That would be a pity. It would cover his face and she really didn't like the feel of a beard against her skin.

Dismayed, she gave herself a mental shake. Where were these thoughts coming from? Hadn't she told herself that she was not interested in David—beard or no beard—or any man, for that matter?

David smiled ruefully. 'Thought it was a puncture and was about to fix it when I saw that the tyre has been shredded.' He pointed to the tyre and Olivia saw what he meant. It looked as if it had been slashed. Perhaps the boyfriend of one of David's conquests had decided on revenge?

'I don't suppose you happen to have a spare in that trunk of yours?' Although he grinned, fatigue dampened the sparkle in his eyes. It was seven in the evening and, like most of the doctors in the hospital, he'd probably been in well before rounds at eight. So he had likely done at least a twelve-hour day, most of which would have been on his feet in Theatre.

'No. I have everything in there—kitchen sink included—except a spare. But I can give you a lift if you like.'

He stood up and stretched. She'd forgotten how tall he was. He topped her five feet seven inches by at least half a foot.

'Would you? That would be great.'

'Jump in,' she said.

She hid a smile as she watched him fold his long legs into the passenger seat. It would be an uncomfortable journey for him, but better than walking or waiting for a cab.

'Where to?' she asked as she pulled out of the car park.

He named a suburb that bordered the one where Olivia lived.

'You're not far from me. I live in Sea Cliff.'

He whistled through his teeth. 'They must pay ER residents better than I thought.'

She decided to ignore his comment. 'I have to make a short detour to pick up my dog, if that's okay.'

'Sure.' He pulled his mobile out of his pocket and flicked through his contacts. 'Will you excuse me for a moment?' He threw a smile in her direction as he pressed the call button. 'Have to cancel my date. She's going to be as mad as hell, but by the time I get washed up we'll have missed the first act.' He grinned. 'Opera's not my style anyway. I would probably fall asleep before the first scene was over.'

She smiled briefly and concentrated on the traffic. His love life was no business of hers.

When he'd finished his call, which, judging by the one-sided version Olivia heard, didn't go down very well until he promised to make it up to her—whoever she was—soon, he turned his attention to her again.

'I suspect Melissa and I are heading for dumpsville. It doesn't matter how often you tell people that your work comes first, they never quite believe it, do they? In that respect, it's easier going out with another medic. At least they understand.'

His words made her think of Richard. He hadn't been in the profession, quite the opposite. He'd been the CEO of a large multinational company, but he'd always understood how important her job was, just as she'd understood that he'd needed to work the hours he had. Perhaps, given their busy schedules, if they hadn't met when they'd still been in college, they would never have ended up together. As it was, she could only regret the hours that they hadn't spent with each other. If only they'd known their time together was going to be so short.

Preoccupied with her thoughts, it wasn't until she pulled up outside the doggy day-care centre that she noticed at some point during the journey David had fallen asleep. God, she knew the need to nap wherever and whenever so well—most doctors learned the knack early on in their careers. In sleep he looked younger and, without the swagger, more vulnerable. He really did need a shave, she thought distractedly, trying not to notice that his lips were full, and even in sleep he looked as if he was on the verge of smiling.

Just as she was about to reach over and give him a small shake, his eyes snapped open and he was instantly alert.

'God, I hope you weren't in mid-sentence when I zoned out?'

'How long were you on duty today?' she asked.

He frowned. 'Dunno. Last time I was home was yesterday morning. I stayed in the hospital last night. I slept in the on-call room for a couple of hours. Between two and four, I think it was.'

'You were on overnight? And during the day too? That can't be good—for you or your patients!'

He quirked an eyebrow. 'Don't you go all mumsy on me. I know my limits. As long as I get a couple of hours' decent sleep, I'm usually fine.'

Mumsy? Had he just called her mumsy?

'I won't be a moment,' she said, and hopped out of the car. When she returned with Bouncer, who looked dismayed to find someone in his seat, David was, once more, out for the count.

Bouncer barked at Olivia apologetically before jumping onto David's lap.

'What the hell…?' David's eyes snapped open again and he pushed at Bouncer, who was clearly not intending to move.

'David, meet Bouncer. Bouncer, meet David.' She

grabbed Bouncer's collar and tried to pull him off David's lap, but the dog was having none of it. A be-mused-looking David took hold of Bouncer, climbed out of his seat and deposited him in the back. 'Stay there,' he commanded.

To Olivia's amazement, her dog, who would never do what she wanted unless bribed and coaxed, looked at David, blinked and lay down obediently.

'How did you manage to do that?'

'Dogs just need a firm hand, just like…'

Please, God, don't let him say just like women and children.

'Just like…' He hesitated. 'Just like horses,' he fin-ished, his eyes glinting. He yawned. 'Think I might close my eyes again, if that's okay?'

'Sure.' Olivia pointed the car in the direction of home and by the time she'd turned into her street David was asleep again.

When she pulled up outside her house, Bouncer leapt from the car. David opened his eyes and looked around sleepily.

'Where would you like me to drop you?' she asked.

'Here's just fine.'

'Are you sure you don't want me to take you all the way? You seem in urgent need of a good night's sleep.'

David hid a yawn behind a fist. 'I am. The truth is that the people I'm staying with—my friend and his wife—have a newborn baby. God! I never knew such a small thing could make so much noise. It's just until I move into my own place. Trouble is that won't be for another three weeks.' He raised an eyebrow. 'Do babies stop crying when they're older? I sure hope so.'

'Not actually having had a baby, or any nieces and nephews, I can't tell you that.' She was clearly in the mother category, as far as David was concerned. Why that should bother her as much as it did, she had no idea.

David stretched languorously. 'Just as well I stayed in the hospital last night, though. Meant I was on the spot to deal with a brain injury from an RTA.' He opened the door. 'Thanks for the lift but I'll run the rest of the way from here. At least being on the move will keep me awake and hopefully by the time I get home the little critter will have gone to sleep. But I sure could do with something to eat first. I don't suppose you know of a place between here and my street?'

Olivia hesitated. She really didn't want to spend any more time in this man's company than she had to. But she recognised a starving, exhausted doctor when she saw one. Whatever and however he made her feel, he was a colleague. He needed food—just as she did—and then bed.

'Look, I was planning to grab some dinner at a place I know just along the road a bit.' She pointed towards the bay. 'How about joining me? I'll give you a lift home after we've eaten.'

'No one waiting for you?' David replied, looking puzzled.

Olivia faltered. She hated having to explain about Richard's death and how she had come to be pregnant with his child, so she'd become adept at sidestepping people's curiosity. 'No, not any more.'

David looked at her searchingly and for a moment she thought he was going probe further. She returned his gaze steadily, willing him not to ask her any more questions. Almost imperceptibly, his intelligent eyes flickered, as if he'd read her mind. And then his by now familiar, lazy grin was back.

He turned his gaze in the direction she had pointed. 'Does this place do steaks? I could murder a T-bone.'

Of course he was a steak man. Could he really be anything else?

'No steaks, but they do a mean chicken pie.'

CHAPTER THREE

Over dinner, chicken pie for him and a salad for her, and with Bouncer snoozing at their feet, they chatted about Mark. David was optimistic that he would make a full recovery.

Finally, he leaned back in his chair. 'Coffee?'

'Not for me. I'll have a herbal tea.'

'Herbal tea! Does no one in this state eat normal food? The Californians don't know what they're missing.' However, he called over the waitress who had been smiling and dancing attendance since they'd walked in the door—the very same waitress, Olivia noted sourly, who normally had to be summoned at least three times before she deigned to attend to *her*. Unsurprisingly, their drinks arrived only moments after David had ordered them.

'Anything else?' the waitress asked, placing her hand on her hip and smiling directly into David's eyes.

'Thank you, but no.'

Olivia hid a smile at the waitress's obvious disappointment. No doubt she'd been hoping to be asked for her number. The look she gave Olivia was less than friendly.

'So,' Olivia asked, 'what made you move from New York, seeing as you like your steaks so much?'

'The job here. I'd have to wait a year for an attending post to come up in New York.'

'This is your first attending position?' She was surprised. He seemed so self-assured when dealing with his patients.

'Yep. Thought I may as well work in sunny Frisco for a year.' As he took a satisfied gulp of his coffee, Olivia couldn't help but notice his long, slim fingers. For a split second she imagined those same hands skilfully dancing along her skin and was instantly horrified. What in God's name was she thinking? She forced herself to concentrate on what David was saying.

'You're not from these parts either, are you? English, I'm guessing. So what brought you to the US?'

She shifted in her seat, still feeling slightly unbalanced by her thoughts of a few moments ago. 'I still have the accent, huh? Even though I've been here for years. My folks came over from London when I was a little girl and settled in Boston. That's where I went to med school.'

'Good choice.' He tipped his head to the side. 'They've got some of the best teaching hospitals. And then you moved out West?'

'That's about it.' Olivia made a show of looking at her wristwatch. 'It's getting late. I'd better get home and Bouncer fed.'

David leaned forward. 'I'm sure Bouncer won't mind waiting another five minutes. What happened after med school?' His eyes held hers, all signs of his earlier fatigue completely gone.

'It's a long story.'

'I have time, and I'd like to hear it.'

Olivia raised her eyebrows. 'Sure you're not stalling

just so that you don't have to go back to your friend's apartment with the crying baby?'

'Well, that's part of it, sure.' His lips twitched when she pretended to look shocked. 'Look, if you don't want to tell me, that's fine by me.'

Olivia studied the man sitting opposite to her. Could he really be interested?

Yet the need to talk about Richard and their life together was strong. Maybe it was the intense way David was looking at her, as if she was the most fascinating woman he'd ever come across. It was dark outside and they were the only people left in the deli. The waitress had dimmed the lights and was huffily tidying up, making it clear that she thought it was time for them to go.

'My husband—Richard—and I got together when we were both at college. We dated and then got married. I was doing my residency and, as you will know from your own experience, working all hours. As was he. He joined a large company and was put on the fast track. It meant we spent little time together, but we were happy. Richard, as expected, shot up the corporate ladder. I got a job at the hospital and I guess we continued as before. We moved to San Francisco when Richard was promoted to CEO of his company.

'Then it became time to think about having a family. We had just started trying when Richard started getting these headaches. At first we put it down to pressure of work—he was busier than ever—but the headaches kept getting worse.'

David's eyes were fixed on hers, his head tipped slightly to one side. She could see that his neurosurgeon brain was way ahead of her, but he said nothing. It was almost uncanny how still he was. Up until now he had been a mass of restless energy despite his evident exhaustion. This was no doubt the kind of focus he brought to surgery.

'Eventually I persuaded him to see someone. You can imagine the number of tests he had to go through. And then, finally, the results.'

Her breath hitched as the memory of the pair of them sitting in the surgeon's consulting room—the pity in his eyes as he'd told them his diagnosis. Imprinted on her memory was the look on Richard's face. First the confusion then the disbelief.

'He was diagnosed with a brain tumour.'

David shook his head. 'I'm so sorry.'

'It was the fastest-growing kind. I knew that Richard had a year, two at the most. I didn't want to tell him the prognosis, but he made me. Richard was the kind of man who had to know exactly what he was dealing with.

'I wanted to put having children on the back burner so we could concentrate all our energy on him—but Richard was determined to store sperm. He wanted to believe that he would be the person who survived the cancer but he knew that the chemo would make him infertile. So that's what we did. We stored his sperm before he started treatment for his tumour.' She shivered and smiled grimly. 'As you can imagine, those were dark and difficult days. It didn't help that Richard wasn't the easiest of patients.'

She looked out of the window. Although over four years had passed since they'd learned of his tumour, it was almost as if she was back in that dark, dark time.

'Against the odds, he went into remission. The chemo shrank the tumour and he was well enough to return to work, as I did. But he was still desperate for us to try for a baby. I guess he suspected it was our only chance of having a child together.

'I went for IVF—not the most pleasant process, as you can imagine—but the first cycle didn't work. Then Richard got sick again so naturally we put the IVF on hold.' She sucked in a breath. 'He died six months later. That was three years ago.'

Something shifted behind David's eyes but Olivia was too caught up in her story to finish now.

'A few months ago, I decided it was time to move on with my life.' She smiled ruefully. 'We had four frozen embryos left. I didn't want to wait until I was in my forties to have a baby, so I went ahead with IVF, using one of the embryos we still had stored.' She tried to keep her voice matter-of-fact, as if she was talking about someone else and not herself. She wasn't going to share her loneliness since Richard had died, or the empty, crushing disappointment she'd felt when the first attempt at IVF had failed. Neither was she prepared to share her constant yearning to hold a baby in her arms and her fear that the second attempt would fail too—especially not with someone who was, after all, a stranger.

But, strangely, David didn't feel like a stranger. Nevertheless, she'd already said too much.

'So *voilà*! I'm pregnant,' she finished. 'Nineteen weeks and counting.'

'And you're doing this on your own?'

'And why not? Thousands of women do.'

'I don't envy you. My friend's baby might weigh only a few pounds, but there's no mistaking who rules the roost in that house.'

Embarrassed that she'd been talking as if she were a leaky bucket, Olivia changed the subject.

'What about you? I assume by the way you're talking that you have no children of your own.'

'Good God, no!' He looked so shocked she almost

laughed. 'Children and I don't quite…go together,' he said. 'And if I ever doubted it, after a couple of weeks at my friend's place, I sure know it now.'

'But you must have children as patients?'

'*That* is entirely different. They're not mine. I don't have to deal with their crying and constant demands. Children and I are not for each other. Don't get me wrong, little Alice is the cutest thing ever, but the best thing about her is that she is not my responsibility.'

'Perhaps when you meet the right woman?'

He looked bemused. 'What is it with women? You all seem to think a person can't be normal if he or she doesn't want children.' He pulled out his wallet and when Olivia made to do the same he shook his head. 'My treat. You were good enough to give me a lift. It is the least I can do.' He yawned. 'But you'll have to forgive me, if I don't get to bed soon, there's every chance I'll be spending the night with my head on this table.'

'Come on, then, I'll run you home. And since I have to go in to work for a couple of hours tomorrow morning I'm happy to give you a lift—if you like?'

He smiled. 'I'd appreciate it. Don't worry about picking me up, though. I'll come to you.'

CHAPTER FOUR

DAVID crept into his friend's flat, grateful to hear nothing but blessed silence. For once the baby seemed to be asleep. Kate had left a terse note about a woman having phoned several times and didn't he know she wasn't his secretary? David groaned. Melissa. She wasn't aware of it yet, but their short dalliance had come to an end. Once a woman started making unreasonable demands, it made him run in the opposite direction as fast as he could.

He opened the fridge and helped himself to an ice-cold beer.

Somehow he couldn't see Olivia hanging onto a man as if her life depended on it. There was something too proud, too self-assured about her, despite—or maybe because of—what she'd been through. She was resilient, no doubt about it.

He sighed as he undressed. In other circumstances she was exactly the type of woman he would have made it his business to pursue. Intelligent, beautiful and, most importantly, independent.

But, of course, any chance of an affair with Olivia was out of the question. The fact that she was a widow would have been off-putting enough—but a pregnant widow? No way. No matter how beautiful, she was untouchable. Which was a pity.

He climbed into bed and pulled the duvet over him. Sleep. He had to be up again in less than six hours, so he had to make the most of every minute.

But just as he was drifting off, a sound like a host of banshees let loose had him sitting bolt upright. Ye gods, what was it? But then as the shrieks settled down into the more recognisable cries of a disgruntled baby, he almost wished the house *had* been invaded by banshees. At least then he could have sent them on their way. He thumped his pillow in disgust and pulled it over his ears. He was so tired, surely not even that racket could keep him awake?

Only it wasn't just baby Alice who invaded his thoughts and prevented sleep but the memory of a beautiful blonde-haired woman with an impish smile and determined eyes.

Olivia was dreaming, lovely dreams where she was lying on a beach with a book in her hand and nothing to do for the rest of the day, when a loud banging on the door woke her up. She glanced at her watch. Six am! Who the hell could it be? Calls at this time usually meant bad news. As she hurried to the door, Bouncer following at her heels, she mentally ran through all the possibilities in her head. Dad was in Boston, surely still asleep at this time, and her best friend was in the UK. Her heart hammering, she opened the door only to find an exhausted-looking David, leaning against the doorjamb, his eyes half-closed. He held out a paper cup to her.

'Good. You're up,' he said, thrusting the cup into her hand before bending down and giving an ecstatic Bouncer a scratch behind the ears. 'I guessed you would be.'

Olivia stared at him, speechless as he walked past

her without so much as a by your leave. He sank into her leather sofa, removed his shoes, and propped his feet up on the table.

'Do you have any idea what time it is?' she spluttered.

'I know exactly what time it is. Just after six. I've been counting virtually every blessed minute since four this morning. Baby Alice—cute as a button but as loud as a banshee—hardly slept a wink, so neither did I. Teething—or so her mother says.'

'I know I said I would give you a lift to work, but I meant at a decent hour. In fact, I distinctly remember us agreeing on seven-thirty!'

Instead of looking embarrassed and penitent, he lay back on the sofa, placed his hands behind his head and eased his legs out in front of him. At least Bouncer had the grace to look guilty as he climbed onto the couch next to David and curled up against him. 'Don't mind me,' David said.' I'm happy to wait until you're ready to go.' He raised an eyebrow and grinned. 'Nice look, by the way.'

She looked down, mortified to find that her breasts were as clear as day under her thin vest that she wore with her pyjama shorts. She'd been so disorientated and anxious to answer the door she hadn't stopped to cover herself.

She was about to grab him by the arm and physically eject him when she noticed his breathing had already deepened. She went to stand over him. Sure enough, he was fast asleep. And so was her dog.

Why, oh, why had she stopped to give him a lift? For some reason he had taken that as carte blanche to invite himself into her life. Was he so used to women keeling over in admiration that it hadn't crossed his mind that his behaviour was completely out of order?

Or maybe the man was mad? Perhaps he'd been removed from his job in New York for irrational behaviour? Perhaps the reputation of California for being more accepting of idiosyncratic personalities had brought him here?

And it was all very well for him to imply that she could go back to bed until later, but once she was up, she was up!

Still seething, she took a sip of whatever he'd brought in the carton. Raspberry tea. It was delicious—but if he thought he was going to get around her with a cup of herbal tea he had another think coming.

She stalked into the study and booted up her computer. A few moments later she typed in David's name.

Immediately several entries came up, mostly articles in *JAMA* with his name attached. So he was definitely a well-regarded neurosurgeon. No evidence of him being struck off for flaky behaviour, then.

But then, a few lines below, another item appeared. One that made her suck in her breath. It was a photograph of David, standing with his arm around a beautiful brunette in front of a nightclub. But it wasn't so much the photograph that surprised her, it was the caption. 'Dr David Stuart, heir to the Stuart fortune, with partner, snapped outside the 40/40 club.'

David—heir to one of the richest men in America?

She clicked away from the page, terrified lest David wake up and find her snooping into his private life. But what was the heir to the Stuart fortune doing, riding to work on a pushbike? And, more importantly, why was a man who could probably afford to buy a hotel, never mind pay for a bed for a few nights, putting up with a screaming infant keeping him awake at night?

* * *

By seven Olivia had showered, dressed, fixed her make-up, taken the traitorous Bouncer for his walk and, with nothing left to do, was fixing some pancakes.

She shrieked when she heard a voice in her ear. 'Something smells delicious.'

She whirled around to find herself almost trapped in the circumference of David's arms as he eyed the pan hungrily.

'And the pancakes smell good too,' he added with a grin.

'If you care to take a seat at the table,' Olivia said pointing in the direction of the dining room, 'I'll bring them in to you.'

'And what's wrong with right here?' David plonked himself down at the kitchen table.

Nothing, she supposed. But all of a sudden the kitchen seemed too small, too intimate.

'What time are you expected at work?' she asked.

'Eight should be early enough. What about you?'

'Actually, no fixed time. I have the day off, although there's some stuff I'd need to attend to at the hospital first. Once I've done that, I can relax and enjoy the rest of the day,' Olivia said pointedly.

'Sorry. I guess you must have wanted to sleep a bit longer. I was walking—anything to get away from the baby crying—and I just happened to find myself near here. Then I saw the light so I guessed you were up.'

'I always leave a light on for Bouncer,' she said. 'He doesn't like the dark.'

David's lips twitched. 'I'll run to work,' he said.

'I might as well drive you since I'm up.' She flipped a couple of pancakes onto his plate. When he raised his eyebrows in mock dismay, she reached inside the fridge for several more eggs and began cracking them into a bowl.

'Seriously, I'm happy to run,' David said. 'I'll shower when I get to the hospital and grab a pair of clean scrubs.'

'I'll take you,' Olivia said firmly. 'Apart from a couple of hours of paperwork I need to finish at the hospital, I don't have anything concrete planned for the day. Besides, I'm curious to see how Mark is doing for myself. I'll come up to the ward with you and then you're on your own.'

David tucked into his breakfast with obvious relish. 'You've got a deal.'

CHAPTER FIVE

THE neuro ward was unexpectedly quiet. Whenever Olivia had been up to see patients in the past it had always been full, but today there couldn't have been more than half a dozen patients in the beds.

As she walked with David to Mark's bed, she noticed a few sly smiles and jabbing elbows from the staff.

Great. It hadn't crossed her mind that arriving together, so early in the morning, would cause gossip and speculation. For the briefest moment she was tempted to march up to the nurses' station and tell them in no uncertain terms that David had not stayed the night. But as quickly as the thought came into her head, she dismissed it. She couldn't care less what anyone thought—she knew the truth. If anyone should be worried about gossip, it should be David.

Mark was still heavily sedated but responding well to stimuli, so David ordered his sedation reduced.

A few beds along from Mark was a little girl who was sitting up in bed with a bandage over her eyes. A soft toy lay on the floor. It had either fallen or been thrown there. There didn't seem to be anyone visiting—perhaps the parents had popped out for a breath of fresh air—and there was something in the little girl's stillness, the way her head was cocked as if listening out for familiar footsteps, that made Olivia's heart ache for her.

She left David writing something in Mark's notes and walked across to the little girl.

'Hello, there,' she said, careful to make her presence known before she spoke. 'I'm Dr Simpson. What's your name?'

The head turned slightly towards her as if seeking out where the voice was coming from.

'I'm Sunny. Have you come to examine me?' The child's voice was resigned. No doubt she was used to being prodded and poked.

'No, sweetheart. But I see you've dropped your teddy on the floor.' Olivia bent down to retrieve the soft toy. She placed it in Sunny's hands.

'I wondered where he'd got to,' Sunny said. 'He's naughty. He doesn't like it here and is always trying to escape. I told him we have to stay. At least for a little while.'

There was a movement beside Olivia as David came to stand next to her.

'Hi, pumpkin,' he said. 'How's your head?'

'That you, David?' Sunny asked. 'I was wondering where you were.' Her mouth pulled into a petulant pout. 'The nurses said you wouldn't be in until later. I told them that you promised to come and see me first, but they wouldn't believe me.'

David? He had his patients calling him by his first name? All her misgivings flooded back.

'I never break my promises, Sunny. I would have been in sooner, but...' He slid a glance in Olivia's direction. 'You know how it is.'

The child giggled. 'Will you read to me?'

'Sure,' David said. 'Only if we get to read the scary

bits again. Man, the part we read yesterday stopped me from sleeping too well last night. What about you? How did you sleep?'

'Not too well.'

'I'm sorry 'bout that. Was it the story or was your head hurting?'

Sunny's smile was tremulous. 'My head.'

'Could you point to where and as you're doing that, remind me where we got to in the story. My memory isn't so good. Was it where the Gruffalo gets lost?'

'No, silly, it was way after that. Don't you remember?'

Olivia smiled as she stepped away. Now she knew what David was doing. He was making an assessment of the child under the guise of just chatting to her. Whatever he said about not liking children, he was doing pretty well with Sunny.

She waited for a little while, watching David with Sunny, curious to know what was wrong with the little girl. She ran a few diagnoses through her head and the one she kept coming back to was a medulloblastoma. That would explain the headaches and the obvious loss of vision. She hoped to hell she was wrong. Her head started to throb. God, nature could be cruel. A brain tumour in a person of Richard's age was bad enough—but in a child? It was too heartbreaking. All of a sudden the ward felt as if it were closing in on her. Being on Neuro brought back too many bad memories.

As she was about to leave, Sunny's parents came in. After they'd greeted their little girl they turned to David with hope in their eyes. David said a few words to Sunny before leading the parents away to speak to them.

There was a lot more to Dr David Stuart than she'd expected, she conceded grudgingly. Now, why didn't that make her feel better?

CHAPTER SIX

'NO WAY, Olivia. Put that idea straight out of your head.'
Kelly dropped the charts on the desk and, picking the
one from the top, turned to a nurse. 'Could you see to
the patient in cubicle three? His stitches from last week
need removing. Then see what you can do about getting
Mrs Lumsden a bed. She's been waiting for two hours.'

'Please, Kelly.' Olivia tried again.' You know you
love Bouncer.'

Kelly harrumphed. 'I might love him but that dog has
no manners. There is no way I'm going to have him in
my house again. Not after the last time.'

'He was only a puppy then. He didn't mean to chew
your husband's slippers. He's much better behaved now.'

'The answer is still no. Find some other stooge. Or
take him with you.'

'You know I can't take him on the plane. Anyway, it's
only for the weekend. You could move into my home.
You're always saying that you could do with a few days'
peace and quiet.'

Kelly eyed her balefully. 'Now, here's the thing. I
might say I want peace and quiet, but I don't really mean
it. I hardly spend any time with Frank as it is.'

Frank was Kelly's husband. The staff joked that he
didn't really exist as no one had ever actually seen him.

'Then bring Frank too. You'll have the run of the house. You can take a swim, watch the sun go down from the beach or just chill.' Olivia wheedled, nudging the box of doughnuts she'd bought on her way in closer to Kelly as an extra incentive.

Kelly sniffed the warm smell of melting sugar and for the briefest moment Olivia thought she'd won her over. But then Kelly pushed the box away. 'Sorry, the answer is still no. Think you can get around me with a few doughnuts? Didn't you know I am on a diet?'

Kelly was always on a diet. Or saying she was. Sugared doughnuts were her downfall. Olivia suppressed the pang of guilt at her pathetic attempt to wean Kelly off her diet and onto the dark side. But she was desperate.

'Anyway, I happen to like my own place. Yours is all very well, but it's not exactly cosy, is it? I'd feel like a pea rattling around in a jar there.' Her voice softened. 'Ask one of the others to house-sit for you. Most of them will jump at the chance.'

'Most of who will jump at what chance?' Olivia hadn't heard David approach, his soft-soled shoes making no sound on the floor.

'Dr Simpson is looking for a house-sitter for her dog. I wish her all the luck with that—she's going to need it.'

'A house-sitter?' David raised his eyebrow. 'For Bouncer? But he's a softie.'

'You've met him?' Kelly's eyes drilled into Olivia's and her lips twitched. 'I didn't know. When?'

'I have to go to Boston for the weekend to see my dad,' Olivia interrupted quickly. Kelly was a sweetheart but loved nothing better than a good gossip—especially if it involved one of her staff. 'I can't take Bouncer with me and I don't want to put him in the kennel. He's got such bad memories from when he was last there.'

She'd acquired Bouncer shortly after Richard had died and when Bouncer had still been a puppy. It had been a reckless move at a time when she'd been feeling lost and lonely, and she hadn't thought through the implications of owning a pet while she was working full time. The truth was that Bouncer had been the unwanted runt of the litter and one look from his soulful, dark eyes had sent any practical thoughts flying from her mind. Now, despite his unruly behaviour, she couldn't imagine life without him. She'd tried to leave him in a kennel once before, but he'd pined terribly, refusing to eat or drink. The next time she'd managed to persuade Kelly to take him, but Bouncer had missed Olivia and regressed to puppy behaviour, chewing everything he could get his teeth into. She simply had to do something about her pet's belief that he was her one and only before the baby came along.

'I could house-sit,' David offered. 'God knows, I could do with a few nights' decent sleep.'

Although she'd seen David in the ER department a couple of times since he'd turned up at her house, she hadn't spoken to him, apart from agreeing treatment schedules for patients.

'You haven't found a place of your own yet?' Odd, when he could surely afford to rent anything he wanted. Of course she couldn't say that. Not without revealing that she knew he was loaded. She tried not to feel miffed that she had practically told him her whole life story yet he'd told her almost nothing about his.

'I've bought somewhere, but it won't be ready for me to move into for a couple of weeks.'

It would be a solution. Bouncer liked David and David was good with him. 'I'm not looking for a guest for a couple of weeks—just a few days.'

'Suits me. A couple of days are all I need.' He yawned. 'Hell, a couple of uninterrupted hours will do.'

A nurse came to ask Kelly something and she moved away.

'Okay,' Olivia said. 'I'd appreciate that. Why don't you come over tonight and I'll show you where to find everything?'

'Tonight?' His eyes brightened. 'I don't suppose I can bring my gear?' He grinned. 'Bouncer should get used to having me there before you go.'

Olivia was still perplexed as to why David hadn't moved out of his friend's and into a hotel, and wasn't at all sure that she wanted to spend a night under the same roof as him. But what harm could it do? His private life was his business and her house was so big it was perfectly possible for two people to share it and almost never bump into each other. Besides, he was right—it would be less stressful for Bouncer this way, and it was only for one night. Her flight to Boston was booked for tomorrow afternoon and she'd be catching the late flight back on Sunday. And after everything she'd been through, a few hours with David was a piece of cake.

True to his word, David arrived that evening with a holdall in one hand and a brown paper bag in the other. Bouncer did what he did best and bounced with delight as soon as he saw his new friend in the doorway.

'I thought I would put you in the guest bedroom on the top floor,' Olivia said. 'I'll show you up.' Naturally she didn't tell him that she'd put him in the bedroom furthest away from hers on purpose. She would rather die than let him know the effect he was having on her. She couldn't go on blaming her hormones for ever, but her heart had given a most definite skip when she'd seen him on her doorstep in his hip-hugging jeans and close fitting black T-shirt. In the three years since Richard had died, no one had ever made her pulse so much as stutter, but she just had to clap eyes on this man and she felt like a schoolgirl with a bad case of the hots. As usual, her timing was impeccable. She was pregnant, for God's sake! And of all the people in the world to be developing a crush on, couldn't she have chosen someone where there was a chance of commitment? Someone less pleased with himself? Less enigmatic?

'Bouncer likes his walks,' Olivia said, hoping that her face wasn't as red as it felt. 'Doggy day care walks him twice a day when I'm working, but when I'm off I take him out three times at least. Once in the morning, once at lunch time and once at night. I'm warning you, you have to hold his leash tightly. I love him dearly, but he's not the best-behaved dog.'

'I can do that. In fact, I go for a run twice a day, so he can come too. That should get rid of some of his energy.' Bouncer had his two massive paws on David's chest and was licking his face ecstatically. 'Down, boy,' David ordered, and to Olivia's astonishment he immediately obeyed. 'I like kisses,' David said with an amused glance at Olivia, 'but I draw the line at doggy ones.'

'Have you had dinner?' Olivia asked, trying not to think what it would like to be kissed by David.

'Picked up some take-away from Chi's Chinese Delight on the way here. Brought enough for two just in case. Left it on the hall table.'

Olivia shook her head. 'I love Chinese, but I'm trying to eat properly.' She tapped her tummy. 'You know.'

David frowned and something in his dark eyes shifted.

'But you're welcome to enjoy it while I fix myself some salad.'

Strangely it felt good to have David in her kitchen. Too good. It was as if his energy had brought the house back to life.

David waited until she had her meal ready before he started on his.

'This is so good,' he said. 'Sure you don't want a taste?'

Olivia had to admit that whatever he was eating did smell delicious. It had been so long since she'd had something that wasn't full of nutrients and good for her that suddenly she couldn't bear it any more. She had to have a mouthful of whatever it was he was having.

'Perhaps just a spoonful,' she said.

David grinned and his fork disappeared into the carton. He twirled for a while before bringing the fork back out, now covered in noodles.

Olivia laughed. 'I'll never get all that into my mouth!'

'Trust me, you will.' He reached across the table. 'Open wide.'

She felt ridiculous as she did as he asked.

It tasted just as delicious as she'd imagined, but at least one noodle had escaped her mouth and was now spilling down her chin. David reached over with his other hand and gently scooped the offending piece of pasta back into her mouth. For a moment that seemed to last for ever, his eyes locked onto hers. They were so grey they were almost silver and held a quizzical expression as if he was asking her a question. But whatever that question was, she wasn't sure she wanted to answer it.

The moment passed as Bouncer placed a paw on her lap, demanding her attention. She swallowed and dabbed at her chin with a napkin. 'Walk time, I think,' she said lightly, as if nothing had just happened between them. Actually, what *had* just happened between them? 'You make yourself comfortable in front of the TV if you like. I heard there was a Giants game on.'

For a second David looked torn. 'If you're going for a walk, then I guess I am too.'

Olivia grinned. 'Don't look so crestfallen. I'll record the game and you can watch it when we get back.'

As always, the seafront was filled with people walking, rollerblading and cycling. The laid-back atmosphere was one of the things Olivia loved about San Francisco. Although you were in a city, it didn't feel like other cities. A short distance from where she lived there were any number of places to walk and even a small beach nearby.

'How do you find San Francisco? Do you miss New York?'

'Hell, no. I mean, I miss some things. I like the bustle, I like that it is always on the go twenty-four seven, but I feel I can breathe here.'

'What do you do when you're not working?' Damn, that was a gauche attempt at getting him to tell her more about himself. She knew pretty well what he did. 'Or not taking someone out?' she couldn't resist adding with a sly sideways look at him.

He met her glance with mock amazement. 'Dr Simpson! Have you been gossiping about my love life?'

She felt herself blush. Of course that wasn't what she'd been doing but, then, she could hardly admit to looking him up on the internet.

'I meant…' Cripes, what had she meant? 'I mean, you're single, you're good looking…' She had to stop right there before she made more of an idiot of herself than she had already—if that was possible. And right at this moment she doubted it.

His grin told her all she needed to know. 'Please, do go on…it's just getting interesting.'

'I think I've said too much.'

He reached over and took her by the shoulders. 'You've not said enough,' he teased. For a spilt second she thought he was going to kiss her and she held her breath. But then he dropped his hands to his sides. 'Come on, let's keep going. I think Bouncer has spotted his girlfriend.'

Later, when they'd retrieved Bouncer from his wooing, and were walking back towards her house, David turned to her.

'You said you're going to visit your father. What about your mother?'

'She's dead,' Olivia said.

'I'm sorry.'

'It's okay. Mum died when I was very young so I hardly remember her.'

'Just you and your father, then? Or do you have siblings?'

'No. Just me and Dad.' She threw a stick for Bouncer, who raced after it, barking joyously. 'I guess that's why I always wanted children of my own. If Richard hadn't died, perhaps we'd have had two or three—maybe more.' She placed her hand on her swelling bump. 'Now it looks like this little one will be an only child—same as me.'

'You haven't had an easy time of it,' David said after a while. 'Losing your mother when you were young, a husband with a brain tumour then a failed IVF attempt. I'm surprised you're not bitter.'

'Oh, I was bitter all right. When Richard became ill— when we got his diagnosis—I was as angry as hell. It wasn't fair. Richard was a good man. What had we done to deserve this? I called my father when Richard was in hospital. I was crying and railing, and it was Dad who calmed me down. He said...' Her voice hitched. 'He said that life wasn't about the hand we were dealt, but what we did with it. He told me I could go on being angry, or I could use that anger to fight for Richard.' She sucked in a breath. 'For a while I was mad with Dad too, but then I realised that he was right. I had no choice but to deal with Richard's illness—to make the most of every minute we might have. And when he went into remission it seemed that thinking positively had worked. I let myself believe that it would be okay and I think Richard began to believe it too. That's when we decided to go ahead with the IVF. Neither of us wanted to wait a moment longer to have children.'

David placed his arm across Olivia's shoulders and pulled her into the crook of his arm. The gesture was so unexpected, so right, it made her throat tighten.

'But the IVF didn't work.'

'Not the first attempt—no. I lost the baby very early—it didn't implant. Although I was expecting it, or at least told myself to expect to go through a couple of attempts, it was still a blow. But Richard was doing so well, it was as if the thought of having a baby was keeping him alive and focussed, so we agreed to have another try when I had recovered.' She shrugged. 'Richard seemed to be doing okay and we let ourselves believe we had time.' She didn't go into detail about those dark days. One minute she and Richard would be filled with optimism, the next thrown into despair like so much jetsam after a storm. 'Then, about six months after the first IVF cycle and just when we were going to have another try, Richard started losing sensation on his right side. I knew straight away the tumour was back. Of course then there was no thought of more IVF, although Richard made me promise that we would have another go—when he was better.' Her lips felt frozen with the effort of not crying.

'You don't have to tell me any more,' David said quietly.

She pulled away from him. 'No, I haven't really talked about it to anyone before—apart from when we talked at the deli, and to Dad.' There was something healing about going over it again. It was as if by talking about it to David she was saying her last, final goodbye to Richard. 'There's not much more to tell. I promised Richard that whatever happened I would try to have our baby. It meant a lot to him that a part of him would go on living. I think he hoped that a baby would give me comfort later. When he died, I couldn't bear the thought of going through a pregnancy without him. To be honest, I was a wreck and it was all I could do to get dressed each day. Dad came to stay for a while. I don't know what I would have done without him. It was he who suggested I go back to work. He knew that I needed something to focus on, apart from Richard's death.'

'Your dad sounds like a great man,' David said.

'He was—still is. He's been both mother and father to me. Some people might think I have no right going ahead and having a baby when I'm on my own, but if Dad could be a single parent and make a good job of it, I knew I could.' She smiled as she remembered. 'When I was a child, I really, really missed my mother. Especially when I fell in love for the first time and he wanted nothing to do with me.' She laughed. 'I was only ten, but it still hurt. Dad didn't laugh at me or try to pass off my hurt as childish. Instead he went out of his way to make me believe that I was beautiful and that one day the boy—Carlos his name was—would find out what he was missing.'

'Your dad was right. The boy clearly had no taste. His loss.'

Olivia shot him a look. 'I was all teeth and glasses back then and—I have to admit—obnoxiously sure that I knew everything.'

'Maybe Carlos was right, then.'

Olivia made to swipe him but before her hand connected, he caught it in his. 'You might have been all glasses and teeth back then, but you do know that you turned into a very beautiful woman? Your father was definitely right about that.'

His words sent a shiver dancing along her spine. But then she told herself not to be ridiculous. Men like David couldn't help themselves. He probably flirted with every woman who crossed his path. Nevertheless, there was something in the way that he was looking at her that made her feel as if she was the only woman he'd ever said these words to before. Blood rushed to her cheeks. Blast the man. Why did he have to be so completely breathtakingly gorgeous? Why did she have to find herself so attracted to him—and why now?

She pulled her hand away on the pretext of picking up another stick to throw for Bouncer and with that, thankfully, the spell was broken.

As they headed back to the house a little later David watched Olivia playing with Bouncer. She was wearing a simple green dress that showed off her long, tanned legs, and with her hair flying loose about her face she appeared more like a carefree teenager than a woman who'd been through so much.

She was, he had to admit, one of the most remarkable women he'd ever met. Despite numerous blows, she refused to stay down. Richard had been a lucky man to have been loved by this woman.

The thought stunned him. For the first time in a very long time he had allowed himself to be drawn into somebody's life, and not because he wanted to get into her bed. He shook the thought away. The realisation didn't make him feel very good about himself.

But was it so bad to like the way his life was? Straightforward, easy and, most of all, unencumbered. Hell, he'd nearly kissed her earlier. Somehow he'd managed to forget that she was pregnant and soon to be a mother. He kept forgetting. In a few months she'd be bringing home a child who would cry non-stop and demand her complete attention. He came out in a cold sweat. People like Olivia with her complicated life and her arrow-like sense of right and wrong had no place in his life. A woman like Olivia should be with a man who loved her unequivocally and for ever. That's what she deserved. And that's what made her out of bounds. He might be selfish but he wasn't a complete bastard.

Olivia Simpson was not for him. Not ever. Except as a casual acquaintance, of course. Soon she would be out of his life, and he out of hers.

As she looked up from where she was crouching next to Bouncer and laughed, his heart lurched. There was nothing wrong with enjoying her company in the meantime, of course.

By the time they got back home Olivia felt inexplicably happier than she had for a long time. David was surprisingly good company, and so easy to talk to that even though she'd only known him for a short while he was beginning to feel like a friend. But she had to remember that friendship was all that could ever be between them. Her crush—if it could even be called that—was bound to disappear. She'd simply been lonely.

As they let themselves in she was laughing at some story David had just finished telling her. But as she locked the door behind them the atmosphere changed. An awkwardness that hadn't been there before suddenly filled the room. It was as if now that they were alone, they were intensely aware of each other.

'I think I'll head off to bed,' she said quickly, annoyed to hear that she sounded breathless. 'But feel free to catch the game on the TV if you wish.'

David touched her on the shoulder and her skin buzzed, each tiny hair on her arm seeming to stand to attention. Damn. His lips twitched almost as if he knew exactly how her body reacted to him. 'It's still early. Why don't you watch it with me?' he invited softly.

Her breath caught in her throat as he looked down at her. 'It's more fun that way,' he added.

She couldn't for the life of her think of a reason to refuse. It was only just getting dark and she didn't want him to think, even for a second, that she found it difficult to act normally around him. 'Okay—half an hour—but then I'm going to my room to read.'

But the half an hour turned into a couple of hours as Olivia became immersed in the game. In between jumping up and shouting at the TV screen, David explained the finer points of baseball—Richard hadn't really been into sport—and when he did, suddenly she found herself unable to tear herself away.

The two teams were neck and neck until almost the end. When the San Francisco Giants scored a home run in the final minutes, Olivia and David jumped up and cheered.

David turned to her and hugged her, lifting her and twirling her around. The feel of his hard body against hers sent a wave of heat from her pelvis to the tips of her fingers and when he placed her back down she could hardly breathe.

He didn't let her go. Instead, he tipped her chin and brought his mouth down on hers. The pressure of his lips on hers sent shock waves spiralling along her nerves, but before she had a chance to react, he lifted his head. For a moment his eyes glittered down at her and she thought he was going to kiss her again, but a split second later his expression dimmed. He dropped his hands and stepped away. 'Sorry. Shouldn't have done that.'

Confused, Olivia didn't know what to say or what to think.

'I told you you'd enjoy the game,' he continued smoothly, as if the kiss hadn't happened. 'Nobody can live in America and not love baseball.'

'I have and I don't.' She was pleased to hear that there was no evidence of her reaction to him in her voice. 'But it's not quite as boring as I thought it would be.'

His gaze shifted to the TV screen and he frowned. The channel had moved on to a chat show and the host was introducing his first guest, the well-known film star Judith Winters.

Olivia had seen her before—who hadn't? But now she was struck by how familiar she looked. She'd seen that full mouth somewhere before and recently. And it wasn't just that. The star had a way of cocking her head to the one side that reminded her of David. She glanced between him and the TV screen.

He was watching it with a far-away look on his face. He stepped away from her and bent to switch the TV off.

'No, David, wait a moment,' Olivia said. She looked

at the actress and then at David. Yes, there was a definite resemblance.

'You're not related to Judith Winters, are you?' She was only joking. Despite the resemblance, it was inconceivable. Besides, he was 'the heir to the Stuart fortune'. He couldn't be both!

'My sister,' David admitted with a wry twist of his mouth. 'One of them.' So he *could* be both. This time he did switch the TV off. He turned to face her and she waited expectantly for him to continue. Perhaps at last she'd find out more about what made this man tick.

'My family,' David continued, 'couldn't be more different from yours if they tried. My family—' He stopped suddenly. 'Aren't worth discussing.' He stood and stretched, his usual open expression dark and closed. 'I think I'll head off to bed, if that's okay.'

He was deliberately shutting her out by making it clear that he didn't want to share anything about his personal life with her. He couldn't have made it clearer that his kiss had meant nothing. Confused by the sudden change in him, Olivia could only nod. She'd come dangerously close to forgetting that this man was the last person on earth she should be falling for.

David stripped off his clothes and climbed between the sheets, reflecting wryly that he was doomed to another sleepless night—not because of baby Susan this time but because of Olivia.

He'd nearly lost it downstairs when her warm, inviting, sensual body had moulded itself against his. For an infinitesimal moment he'd been tempted to make love to her. Maybe she wouldn't have regretted anything in the morning, but he would have. Eventually his feelings for her would wane, as they always did, and he'd have taken something from her and given nothing in return.

Seeing Judith on the TV screen had been a timely reminder. He didn't do families or relationships. It was just how he was, the creed he lived by—love lightly, commit to no one and, to avoid hurting anyone too much, move on quickly.

And he knew that when Olivia loved, she would love deeply and for ever. The woman had been through enough. As he listened to the sounds of her getting ready for bed, he realised one thing. No one's good opinion had ever mattered to him as much as Olivia's did. He thumped his pillow in disgust. So what the hell was he going to do about it?

CHAPTER SEVEN

THE next morning she was putting away her breakfast dishes when David walked into the kitchen wearing a pair of jeans and nothing else. His hair was still wet and little droplets of water clung to his chest. She hadn't slept well last night. Images of the brief kiss they'd shared had kept coming back into her head, and she knew she would have kissed him back if he hadn't pulled away. If anything, her ridiculous crush on him was getting worse, but she would rather die than let him know. Casual indifference was what was called for.

'Morning...' He yawned. 'Gee, do you always get up with the birds?'

'Been up, had breakfast, taken Bouncer out for his walk, tidied my wardrobe...' Then she grinned. 'Actually, I'm lying about the last part. I usually sleep in on a Saturday, but I've a plane to catch later, if you remember.'

'I'm going into the hospital, otherwise I'd have taken you.'

'What? On the back of your bike?'

David looked a little sheepish. 'I do have a car, just don't use it all that much.'

'So that morning when you turned up here looking for a lift...'

'I was taking advantage. Sorry.' But he didn't look at all sorry. 'I planned to fix my bike and it wouldn't have fitted in my car.'

She pushed a bowl of oats in his direction. 'If you want some breakfast, that's all I have, I'm afraid.'

He raised his eyebrows in horror. 'No way. I'll pick something up on the way to the hospital. Just coffee will be fine for now.'

'Do you have surgery? On a Saturday?'

'We were supposed to do the operation yesterday, but an earlier case took longer than we thought so we rescheduled for this morning.'

'What it is?'

'I'm operating on Sunny. She has a medulloblastoma.' Olivia wished she hadn't asked.

'What are her chances?'

David grinned. 'With me operating? Good to excellent.' Then he grew serious. 'I wouldn't operate if I wasn't almost a hundred per cent convinced I could remove the bulk of the tumour. It will come back eventually, but this way we'll give her and her parents more time.'

'But removing the tumour could leave her with residual brain damage.' Memories of Richard's illness— the operation he'd had when surgeons had thought there had been a chance of removing the tumour, the realisation after waiting for seven long hours that they hadn't been able to remove it all, then the months of chemotherapy followed by a period of being well, only for the tumour to grow back. She wouldn't wish it on anyone, especially not a little girl.

David was watching her. 'If we do nothing, the tumour will carry on growing. Sunny's already lost most of the vision in her right eye. I'll do everything I can to make her immediate future better, Olivia. That I will promise.' For once there was no trace of his usual bantering tone. 'I suspect you think I don't take anything seriously, and to a certain extent you're right. But one thing I never joke about is my work. I'm good at what I do. Damned good. If there is any way of getting that tumour out without damaging the brain, I'll find it.'

'Can I watch?' she asked, taking herself by surprise. 'My plane doesn't leave until this afternoon.'

David shrugged. 'Sure, if you like. I hope to have her back in the ward by lunchtime.'

Olivia watched the operation from the viewing gallery. David barely acknowledged her presence apart from a brief nod. From the moment he'd stepped into the operating room, he'd seemed to have gone somewhere inside himself.

Sunny, already anaesthetised and intubated, was lying on the table, covered apart from the area where David would be operating. Olivia knew only too well the terror and anguish the little girl's parents would be experiencing right now.

Totally focussed, David used the operating microscope to see what he was doing as he removed part of Sunny's skull. Then, using tiny instruments, he carefully cut through the meninges until the brain was revealed. Every action was displayed on a large monitor with perfect clarity as he manoeuvred part of the normal brain tissue away until he'd exposed a mass of grey tissue, which was the tumour. Very gently, piece by piece, he sucked the tumour away until there was only normal brain tissue left. Satisfied he'd removed as much of the abnormal tissue as he could, he irrigated the wound and did a final check for bleeding, before watching as his resident closed.

By the time he'd finished, Olivia was bathed in a film of perspiration. The operation had taken three hours. If she felt mentally and physically exhausted, how must David feel?

He pulled off his mask and glanced up at the viewing gallery. He caught her eye and grinned, giving her a thumbs-up, before turning his attention back to Sunny. Olivia sat back and let out a whoosh of air. Her heart was hammering.

She was impressed with David's skill. She was impressed with his concentration and with the easy manner he had with his team.

Impressed—that was it.

Not falling for him. No way.

Because that would be crazy.

CHAPTER EIGHT

On the plane, during her visit to her father and, if she was honest, the whole weekend Olivia couldn't stop thinking about David. She kept remembering the way he'd smiled at her, the way he'd grasped her hand, the look on his face after he'd kissed her. In fact, she found herself replaying almost every moment they'd spent together so far.

Not even her father's news, the reason why he'd asked her to make the trip, did more than distract her for short periods.

Her father was getting married again.

Olivia should have been surprised—after all, Dad had been a widower for almost thirty years, and had never shown the slightest interest in dating, never mind marrying again—but she wasn't. He'd been evasive over the last few months when she'd asked him what he was doing with his time, and the last couple of times she'd suggested she take a trip to see him, he'd put her off. She'd wondered if he'd met someone, and she was delighted to learn that he had. Now she wouldn't have to worry about him so much.

'You don't mind, sweetheart?' he asked anxiously, when he'd given her the news as soon as they were home. 'I've been lonely. I don't mind telling you. Perhaps it's because your mother and I had such a good marriage that it seems right to marry again.' He looked at her from the corner of his light blue eyes. 'What about you? Do you think you'll marry again?' He passed her a mug of coffee. 'Raising a child on your own isn't easy, my love.'

'I know. So every one keeps telling me. But I've been waiting for this so long, I don't care if this baby keeps me awake for years. I'm going to enjoy every second of it. You've been both Mum and Dad to me since Mum died, and that worked out all right, didn't it?'

Her father's eyes filled. He'd never been the strong, silent type. 'You know I couldn't be prouder of you, but it doesn't mean that it wouldn't have been easier if there had been two of us.'

Olivia knew he was thinking back to her teenage years when she had rebelled against his gentle but firm hand. She hadn't always been the dutiful, hard-working daughter. Thankfully the phase hadn't lasted long.

As always, her father seemed to know what she was thinking. 'The fact that you went through a difficult phase yourself will help you to be a good mother. You'll know that if you just hang in there, these things usually work themselves out. It's just a shame Richard won't be with you.'

Olivia hugged her father. 'But don't you see, Dad, this way he'll always be with me.'

Her father wiped his eyes. 'You didn't answer my other question—the one about meeting someone else. It's been three years since Richard died, love. Isn't it time?'

'Now, Dad, do you honestly think any would-be suitor is going to want to date a pregnant woman?' Glinting, grey-blue eyes and a teasing grin flashed into her head. *Especially not someone as footloose and fancy-free as David.* 'I have enough on my plate as it is. Between work, Bouncer and preparing for this baby, I've no time for anything else, and when the baby arrives I'll have even less time.' She felt a pang. Although she could never ever regret the baby, perhaps in another time and place something might have developed between her and David.

She tried to push the thought away but it wouldn't go. Was it so very impossible? She and David were very different—that was true—but it didn't make them incompatible. She knew now that he wasn't simply the shallow womaniser she'd taken him for originally but a more complex man. He was also a dedicated and skilled surgeon, so they had medicine in common. And they enjoyed each other's company. More importantly, she knew he was attracted to her. She might not have dated for years, but a woman just knew.

Okay, so she was carrying another man's child, and some men might find that weird, but she wouldn't be pregnant for ever. She wasn't that crazy to think that she was in love with David—or he with her—but who knew what the future might bring?

A warm glow started somewhere in the region of her heart and spread quickly throughout her body. The future looked bright. Very bright.

She turned her attention back to her father. 'So, Dad, tell me everything. When is the big day? When can I meet Jennie? Has she got children?'

It was late on Sunday evening by the time she arrived back home. With a sense of happy anticipation Olivia let herself into her home, wondering, as Bouncer skidded around the corner towards her, if David would be pleased to see her too. She'd caught an earlier flight as thunderstorms had been forecast for the evening and she hadn't wanted to take the chance of being stuck indefinitely at the airport. She lowered her overnight bag to the floor, tossed her car keys into the basket and went in search of him. Her breath caught in her throat as she heard the murmur of voices—one distinctly female, and clearly in distress—coming from the kitchen.

A feeling of dread and disappointment crept along her spine her as she entered the room. David's back was to her but she recognised the tear-streaked face of the brunette who had her arms wrapped intimately around his neck and who was now looking over his shoulder directly at Olivia.

'Please, Melissa…' David groaned, clutching at her hands. 'You have to leave. We can meet tomorrow…' As Melissa released him, something in her expression must have alerted him that they were no longer alone. He swung round and the colour left his face.

'Olivia!' He looked as guilty…as if they'd been in bed together.

'Hello, David. And hello, Melissa. It is Melissa, isn't it?' Olivia said evenly, relieved to hear her voice sounded casually friendly. 'Why don't you continue your conversation in the sitting room while I make us something—?' She stopped abruptly as she took in the unopened French champagne bottle and the two gold-rimmed glasses on the granite countertop. Not hers. Melissa's, then. Brought for an intimate evening. A celebration of sorts. 'Oh, champagne…' Her words petered out. She didn't for the life of her know how to continue.

'Melissa was just leaving, weren't you?' David said, thrusting Melissa's clutch bag into the momentarily disconcerted woman's arms. Her expression changed to one of malice as she glanced at Olivia.

'Of course, darling. Tomorrow, then, like you said?'

'Tomorrow.' David turned to Olivia, his face deadpan. 'I'll just show Melissa out. Back in a sec.'

'Please,' Olivia said sweetly, 'take all the time you need.' She flicked on the kettle and hid her tear-stung eyes in the cupboard as she searched for a cup.

Clearly her early arrival had rained on his parade. Damn him. At the very least he shouldn't be entertaining guests in her home. He was quite rightly embarrassed, and if he was returning to apologise she wasn't going to make it easy for him.

He paused in the doorway, as if as much at a loss for words as she was. It didn't help that he looked disturbingly gorgeous with shower-wet hair and the dark denim of his shirt matching his eyes. She couldn't help noticing that one of the top buttons was in the wrong hole. She stared at it pointedly as a wave of jealousy made her mean. 'I'm sorry if I interrupted anything. If you hurry, you can still catch her…'

'It's not what you think…'

'It really doesn't matter what I think, does it, David?'

'I didn't invite her here. She must have followed me from the hospital. She won't accept it's over. I'm beginning to think she's crazy.'

'Now, now, David. Is that any way to talk about your girlfriend?'

'Melissa and I dated once or twice, but she's not my girlfriend. Whatever ideas she may entertain that we have a future, she's badly mistaken. I can't make it any clearer than I have.'

Hope surged for a moment. But then common sense prevailed: how could she have thought for one moment that a serial philanderer could ever be a part of her and her baby's lives? With the number of women he had begging for his attention, could he ever settle for just one woman? Be faithful for any significant length of time, never mind for ever? It was almost laughable.

He moved closer to her. 'I can't have you thinking that I'd make love to a woman here. *Here?*' His tone was incredulous 'In *your* home? I couldn't, wouldn't, do that.'

She found herself staring at his mouth. How beautiful it was. The top lip so sensual in its curves and width, its corners upturned as if laughter was never far away.

He raised long fingers to her cheek and his touch broke the spell. She flinched and his hand dropped away.

'I should leave,' he said.

'Yes. You should.'

And he did, taking her fleeting moment of happiness with him.

Over the next few weeks Olivia only saw David when he was called down to the ER department for a consult. He would smile briefly at her and was always ready to discuss patients, but apart from that it was as if they'd never spent time together. She'd heard he was dating—most of the female staff had been out with him or were hoping to be asked—but David didn't seem to be settling on any one particular woman. Melissa's name was certainly never mentioned.

She'd also heard that David returned to New York every second weekend without fail, and it was rumoured that he had a girlfriend there. Olivia tried hard not to feel disappointed, but she was. She told herself that it was nothing to do with the fact that she hated to think of David with another woman but rather that she had expected more from the man she had begun to know—or who she had *thought* she'd begun to know. What did she know about him anyway? Not a lot. Only that he had a sister who was famous, that he'd been brought up in New York and liked to date beautiful women. A lot of beautiful women, it had to be said.

No, she'd had a crush on him, but that was in the past, where it would stay.

CHAPTER NINE

'MAN, what is up with you? You look like hell.'

'Thank you, Kelly, for those heart-cheering words.'

'No seriously, Olivia, you look as if you've spent the night walking through the desert or something.'

Neither Kelly's words nor her sharp gaze reassured Olivia one little bit. The truth was she wasn't feeling great. But she *was* twenty-eight weeks pregnant and still working full tilt in the unit. She sighed. Judging by the admissions board, today was going to be a cracker too.

But as she went to collect the charts of her patient, a forty-year-old with a suspected MI, Kelly took up a stance in front of her, blocking her way.

'Uh-uh. No work, honey, until I'm sure you're fine. We have a perfectly good obstetric department just two floors up. I'm going to give upstairs a call and ask them to get you checked out.'

When Olivia started to protest, Kelly whisked the charts out of her hands and gave her a gentle shove towards the lifts. 'You may be the doctor, honey, but everyone knows I run this department. Now get yourself up there, stat.'

Grumbling to herself, Olivia did as she was told. She knew Kelly wouldn't allow her to work unless she was happy that she was fit. Under that fierce exterior, Kelly was like a mother hen, treating all the staff like her baby chicks.

The truth was she had been thinking of calling her ob/gyn consultant to see if he could squeeze her in over at his practice in Hillsborough. Over the last twenty-four hours the baby hadn't been moving as much as usual. She'd told herself that that was normal, but nevertheless it would be good to be reassured. She might be a doctor, but in every other way she was just another first-time mum-to-be.

Dr Washington, a kindly man with grey hair and a small, old-fashioned moustache, insisted on giving her a scan when she explained.

'It won't hurt to do one, Dr Simpson,' the obstetric attending said, 'then we can all feel happier. I'll leave you with Marcella, our sonographer, and we can have a talk afterwards.'

Marcella, a cheerful woman in her early fifties, took her into the dimly lit scanning room. But a few minutes after Marcella put the probe on Olivia's tummy she frowned. 'I'll just get Dr Washington,' she said, and before Olivia could ask what was wrong had scurried out of the room.

Feeling a little sick with anxiety, Olivia turned the monitor to face her and squinted at the screen. Her heart melted as she saw the tiny limbs of her baby on the frozen image, but seconds later her heart jumped into her throat. Something was wrong with the picture. There was too much fluid around the baby—at least, that's how it seemed to her. She propped herself onto her elbows and scrolled through the images. They were so clear she could make out her baby's tiny fingers and even his nose and mouth. She hadn't wanted to know the sex of her baby, but she could tell from one she was going to have a boy. A son! Josh! Josh was the name they'd decided if it was to be a boy. Would he look like Richard?

She peered closer. Was there too much fluid, or was she just being over-anxious? She wasn't an expert at looking at scans but Marcella had clearly seen something that had bothered her.

She was still staring at the screen when a concerned-looking Dr Washington returned with the sonographer.

'Marcella isn't happy with the some of the pictures she's taken and wants me to check them. If you don't mind, I'd like to go over everything from the beginning.'

So there definitely was something wrong.

'What is it?' Olivia demanded, her heart thudding painfully.

'Let me finish having a look, Doctor, then we can talk.'

Olivia wanted to scream with frustration but she forced herself to stay quiet. The sooner she let Dr Washington get on with what he needed to do, the sooner she would have answers.

The obstetric attending spent a few minutes measuring the baby's head, legs and abdomen while murmuring to Marcella that he agreed with her findings. Olivia strained to hear what findings he was talking about in particular, but Dr Washington spoke too quietly for her to make out his actual words.

Eventually, when Olivia thought she was going to explode with fear and frustration, he turned to her. Straight away she could tell from his expression that her instinct had been right. Something was badly wrong.

'I don't know how much you know about obstetric scanning, but if you look at your son's head...' he turned the screen back towards her and pointed '...there's a lot of fluid under his skin that shouldn't be there.' He repositioned the scan probe. 'And if you look around the baby's heart and here in the abdomen, there's a lot of fluid as well.'

It felt as if all the blood from her body had drained away. 'Are you telling me my baby has hydrops?'

'Yes. That's right.'

Olivia was stunned. This was very bad news. Hydrops was a potentially fatal condition.

'It's almost certain that your son is anaemic. When this reaches a serious level the baby's heart has to work extra-hard to compensate and the baby develops a degree of heart failure. It is quite a serious problem, I'm afraid.'

Olivia was struggling to make sense of what Dr Washington was saying. How could her baby be so ill? Dear God, how could this be happening all over again? Hadn't she had more than her fair share of bad luck?

'I'm going to check the blood flow in the baby's brain as well.' He moved the probe back over the baby's head and fiddled with more buttons on the scanner. 'Now I need to do some further tests to find out why the baby's anaemic. Can I have your permission to check your charts from your regular ob/gyn? In the meantime I should take some blood from you.'

After he'd taken blood he left her alone again.

Olivia felt dizzy. Memories of Richard's diagnosis were hurtling around her head. She'd felt the same sense of disbelief and outrage then—the same sense that this could not be happening to her. An unexpected surge of anger flooded through her. Damn Richard for leaving her. Damn him for making her face this on her own. Then, like a wave in a sea storm crashing onto rocks, terror washed over her and she buried her face in the pillow so no one would hear her cries of pain and fear.

By the time Dr Washington returned she'd managed

to regain some control. She was on her own, and as her dad said, it wasn't the hand you were dealt but it was what you did with it that mattered. She would be calm and focussed and would do whatever was required to save her baby.

'First things first,' he said. 'Your baby *is* seriously anaemic and we need to arrange to get him transfused as soon as we can.'

Olivia knew the only way they could transfuse her baby was in utero. It wasn't a straightforward procedure by any means, and it did nothing to reduce the terror Olivia was barely keeping under control. Some babies didn't survive the procedure.

She took a deep breath. *Keep calm. You have to keep calm. Imagine you are discussing a patient. Deal with one problem at a time.* 'Why should my baby be anaemic?'

'This is what we have to find out. There's no sign of any infection in your blood. That would lead me to think of Kell antibodies. I see from your chart that you're Kell negative but also that your husband was Kell negative too, so it shouldn't have been a problem for your baby.'

Olivia fastened on Dr Washington's words. Kell antibodies? That was, as he said, impossible.

She had been tested—an antibody screen was routine for every pregnant woman, and she'd had it as part of her IVF work-up. When she was found to have the Kell antibodies, Richard was tested. If he'd been Kell positive too that would have caused serious risks to the pregnancy—such as fetal anaemia—the condition her baby had. But thankfully Richard's blood group was Kell negative. So that ruled that out.

'We were checked,' she told Dr Washington. 'Richard was definitely negative.'

'Are you sure?'

'One hundred per cent. It's not the kind of thing I would make a mistake about.'

Dr Washington studied the chart in his hand. 'That is what it says here, but I needed to ask.' He cleared his throat and looked a little embarrassed. 'And the baby you are carrying is definitely the result of the embryo transplant? It's not possible that you fell pregnant naturally, by another partner?'

Despite everything, Olivia had to smile. She'd not been on so much as a date since Richard had died, never mind sex with anyone else. 'No,' she said quietly. 'The baby I'm carrying is definitely Richard's.'

'In that case, we'd better check for other antibodies. We'll admit you in the meantime so that we can monitor the baby and arrange the transfusion for tomorrow.'

He patted her on the shoulder. 'I know this is rough, but try not to worry. One way or another, we'll get to the bottom of it.'

He paused as he headed out of the door. 'Is there anyone we could call for you? Someone who could be with you?'

Olivia shook her head. Her best friend was in the UK and pregnant herself. And Dad, well, he was in Boston. Of course he'd come like a shot if Olivia asked him to, but she didn't want to spoil his recent happiness. Besides, what could he do?

Left alone again, Olivia tried to make sense of what was happening. Her baby, her precious baby, was seriously ill and they didn't know why.

While she waited she phoned Kelly to tell her that there was a problem and that she wouldn't be back at work for a couple of days.

'Olivia, what's the matter?'

'The baby is anaemic. They want to transfuse him tomorrow.'

The long pause at the other end of the line told her that Kelly knew exactly how serious that was.

'I'd come up to see you but we have an RTA coming in and with you off duty...'

'Of course, you can't leave the department,' Olivia said firmly, although she would have given anything for Kelly's down-to-earth company right now. 'Don't worry about me. I'll be fine.'

David was heading out of the ER department when Kelly stopped him.

'Dr Stuart, could I have a moment?'

'Sure. Is there someone you'd like me to see?' He liked the head ER nurse. She was unflappable and seemed to anticipate what the doctors required almost before they knew it themselves. The nurses under her were equally professional, although the female nurses flirted outrageously whenever he was around. In fact, one of the nurses whom he'd taken out once before was currently standing behind Kelly and shooting mischievous glances his way. David grinned back. Maybe it was time to ask her out again. She'd been good, undemanding company on their last date. Since that night in Olivia's home when he'd almost kissed her, he'd thrown himself back into the dating scene, knowing that if he didn't he wouldn't be able to stop himself from dropping in to see Olivia. Despite everything he'd told himself, he'd been unable to get her out of his head, and it took all his self-control to keep away from her.

'Well, in a manner of speaking.' Kelly seemed unusually sombre even for her and the tone of her voice made

David focus all his attention on her. 'I sent Dr Simpson upstairs to see the ob/gyn attending earlier.'

David was immediately alert. 'Why?' He hadn't spoken to Olivia except to discuss patients since that day at her house. Although he'd told himself it was better, much better, for both of them that they keep their relationship professional, he found himself straining to catch a glimpse of her blonde head whenever he was in the department—and when he did, he always felt something shift in his chest. Which meant he was doing the right thing by avoiding her. But that didn't mean he didn't want to know she was okay.

'She looked like hell and when I pressed her she admitted she was worried that the baby didn't seem to be moving as much as he has been lately.'

'And?'

'Well, she's just phoned down to say that she won't be able to work for a couple of days. The baby is anaemic so they're going to do an in utero transfusion.'

'Hell.' He could hardly believe what he was hearing. This sounded serious. Hadn't Olivia been through enough?

'And she's up there on her own,' Kelly said. 'I would go and be with her, but there's an RTA coming in. I have to stay here until everyone's been dealt with.'

'I'm on my way,' David called over his shoulder, already moving towards the stairs. 'If you need me you know where to find me.'

When there was a knock on the door, Olivia was certain it was the nurse come to take her to the ward. But to her astonishment it was David who strode into the room.

'Kelly called me to the ER to see a patient. When I was finished she told me you'd come up here hours ago and that they were keeping you in. So, as I had nothing better to do, I thought I might as well look in on you in case there was something wrong. Kelly told me you weren't feeling so good.' Although his words were casual, his eyes were searching her face with the same intensity she'd seen when he was operating.

Of all the people to come looking for her, David was the last person she'd expected but, funnily enough, the one she was most relieved to see. He would be calm and rational where others who knew her better might make her more anxious. There was something so reassuring about his tall, substantial presence that it made her want to cry all over again.

'Kind of helps that one of the nurses is on the lookout for me,' David continued with a small smile. 'Seems to think I promised to take her to dinner—so it kind of gives me a place to hang out.'

Any warmth Olivia was feeling towards him disappeared. 'I am not your decoy. If that's the reason you're here, you might as well leave.'

'I'm here,' he said quietly, all traces of his smile vanishing, 'because I thought you might need a friend.'

The lump in her throat threatened to choke her and she swallowed hard.

'So…' He sat down on the bed, ignoring her outburst. 'What exactly are they saying?'

She explained everything she'd been told, but it didn't make any more sense when she repeated it.

'The samples must have been mixed up.' Her mind latched onto the possibility. They had the samples mixed up and her baby did not have Kells. But there *was* something wrong with her baby. He definitely had anaemia. She wasn't so bewildered that she didn't know that much.

'If my baby needs a blood transfusion, that's not great, is it?' she continued, searching David's face.

'No,' he said, and she winced at his honesty. 'But they're used to doing it here. You have to trust them.' He looked thoughtful. 'I suppose there might have been a mix-up somewhere. I don't think you should worry too much until they check the blood results again.'

But he didn't sound convinced. He started pacing the room with the same restless energy he always seemed to have.

She dug her elbows into the couch and pushed herself into a sitting position.

'Talk to me,' she said. She needed a distraction. There was no point in speculating until the results of her blood tests came back.

He raised an eyebrow. 'What about?'

'Tell me anything. What it was like for you as a child—no, forget that.' She didn't want to think about anything that would remind her of her current situation. 'Tell me why you went into neurosurgery.'

A look of relief crossed David's face. He propped his long legs on the side of the couch and wrapped his arms behind his head.

'Remember Meccano,' he said.

Olivia frowned. 'Meccano? What does that have to do with neurosurgery?'

'When I was a kid I used to love putting all the bits together. Each piece had its exact place. And you had to be so careful not to let your fingers shake because if you did they'd come tumbling down. Then when I was at school, we studied the brain as part of our science course. In many ways it reminded me of my Meccano set. But more interesting. They told us about Phineas

Gage—you know, the guy with the metal rod through his head?'

Olivia nodded. 'Everyone knows about him.' In the corners of her mind dark thoughts kept forming, but as long as she concentrated on what David had to say she could just about keep them away.

'I thought it was so cool that damage to the brain in one area could leave someone relatively unaffected. It was like a giant puzzle to me. The way that if one part was damaged, another bit could come to its rescue. And that very precise bits have very precise functions and even now we still don't know a fraction of what there is to know about the brain. We've explored space, we've conquered the poles, but we hardly know anything about the main organ we all share.'

Olivia hadn't really thought about it. Of course she had studied neurology and the brain as part of her medical degree, but it didn't fascinate her the way it clearly fascinated David.

'Every time I lift a scalpel to operate, it's like I'm conquering my own South Pole. One slip, one messy cut and I could leave someone brain damaged—or worse. On the other hand, my hands can work magic. Just like building a Meccano model I can put someone back together again. Not always, of course—some damage is too great—but often enough to make me feel it is all worthwhile.'

'Sounds to me that you have a touch of the God syndrome,' she teased.

He wasn't offended. 'Don't we all? Isn't that what we do every day of our lives? Try and beat nature with the force of our wills and our skills?'

'Like IVF,' Olivia said. It was no use. She couldn't stop thinking of her own situation. 'Some people think fertility treatment interferes with nature.' She dismissed the thought with a shake of her head. Her baby was *not* ill because he was an IVF baby.

'I'm not a churchgoer,' David said. 'But I do believe that if God does exist he gave us the skills and knowledge we have, whether it's to create babies in a test tube or to save someone's life who would have died without our intervention. It wouldn't make sense not to use them—talents remaining buried and all that.'

Of course he was right. All the doctors she knew believed the same thing.

'I have to stay in overnight so they can keep an eye on the baby. I don't suppose you could…'

'Collect Bouncer and stay at your place with him? Sure. It will be my pleasure.'

At least that was one, easily manageable problem out of the way.

David was sitting on the edge of her bed, doing a crossword, when a nurse came in to take some more blood—for cross-matching this time. Given that the nurse was a raven-haired, long-limbed beauty, Olivia was fully expecting David to turn the full wattage of his smile on her. But to her surprise he didn't. Instead, he stood over her shoulder, watching as she expertly drew blood.

'Did I manage that to your satisfaction, Doctor?' the nurse said curtly when she'd finished.

'Perfectly well,' David said, completely unabashed.

'Surprised you didn't ask her out while you were at it,' Olivia said when the nurse had left the room. She didn't want to think of what was going on around her. She needed distraction.

'Already did. Discovered she's engaged. Fiancé plays

for the American football team. Has shoulders as big as the Green Giant's, so I've decided to pass.'

'Haven't you ever been in love?' Olivia asked.

David grinned at her. 'I'd have to think about that.'

'Then you haven't been. You'd know.'

They both turned as the door opened again and Dr Washington came back in. There was no smile on the elderly doctor's face, no sheepish look as he walked towards them, an apology forming on his lips. There was none of that. Just a grim absolute certainty. He acknowledged David with a terse nod. If he was surprised to see him, he didn't show it.

'Your latest blood test shows a very high level of anti-Kell antibodies, higher than at the start of the pregnancy. This makes it very likely that you are carrying a Kell-positive baby. That would trigger the rise in antibody levels and also explain the baby's condition,' Dr Washington told Olivia.

Olivia shook her head. 'It's impossible. You should repeat the tests.'

The obstetrician sat down beside her and took her hand. 'We are checking the results again, but I have to be honest—I expect the same thing to come back. In the meantime, the transfusion will go ahead as planned tomorrow. Your baby will probably need to be transfused again in a couple of weeks, and we will almost certainly have to deliver him at thirty-four weeks.'

'At thirty-four weeks?' Olivia was dismayed. 'Can't we wait until later?'

'We even considered delivering you now. At twenty-eight weeks most babies have a chance of doing quite well. But we decided against it given that your baby is so premature and also unwell.'

Olivia closed her eyes. Her son was to be transfused,

and if that wasn't bad enough, if he survived, they were going to deliver him early. Her poor, poor baby.

'Would you like me to stay?' Olivia had almost forgotten David was in the room.

'No. You have work to do.' But she did want him to stay. She needed someone to tell her she wasn't going mad, that she hadn't stumbled into some bizarre nightmare. If the blood test on the baby confirmed her results then there was only one other explanation. Somehow in the IVF clinic Richard's sperm must have become mixed up with someone else's. It wasn't supposed to happen—there were safeguards, hundreds of them, to prevent it. So no—she wouldn't even think of the possibility until the second load of results came back.

David got to his feet. There was a strange, almost panicked look in his eyes, as if he was wondering how he'd managed to get caught up in a drama that had nothing to do with him. Then he cocked his head to one side and sat down again. 'Nope. I'm staying. Seems to me you still need a friend. The ward can page me if they need me.'

For a crazy moment Olivia wanted to laugh. However she saw David, it wasn't as a friend. Nevertheless, there was something comforting about the way he folded his arms and leaned casually back in the chair.

He turned away and looked out of the window as Dr Washington wrote in Olivia's chart. Then they were left alone again.

'I'm sorry to have dragged you into this,' Olivia said.

He smiled wryly. 'Whatever you might think of me, I'm not the kind of man to let a woman go through a difficult time on her own.'

Olivia sank back on her pillow. Only yesterday she had been planning her baby's arrival, secure in the knowledge that in a few months she would have her child. Now she didn't know if her son would live—or even whether he was actually hers and Richard's.

But the baby had to be hers. For twenty-eight weeks he had been growing inside her. She'd followed every second of his growth mentally in her head and had known exactly when his heart had started beating, when his lungs had finished developing, when his toenails and fingernails had been forming. It didn't matter what anyone said, this baby was hers.

David looked relieved when a few minutes later they came to fetch Olivia to take her to the ward. 'When will they do the transfusion?' he asked the nurse.

'In the morning some time. We haven't got an exact time yet.' The nurse glanced at David. 'Is he your partner?' she asked Olivia. 'He'd be welcome to be there if he is. Most women find that they can do with the moral support.'

David looked as if he was about to shake his head, but when he glanced at Olivia whatever he saw in her eyes made him hesitate. The thought of the transfusion terrified her, and she didn't want to go through it on her own. She would be sedated throughout, and although she trusted the doctors completely it would be good to have a disinterested party there who could speak for her should she be unable to speak for herself.

'What time?' he asked.

The next morning Olivia lay on her hospital bed not daring to think about the consequences if the transfusion didn't work. Even if it did, her baby—and there was no way she could think of him as anything else—could still have ongoing health problems. But first things first. Right now she had to get through the next forty-eight hours. She'd slept badly. Kelly had come up to see her when she'd finished her shift and although she tried to be reassuring they both knew that the procedure was risky. The transfusion meant putting a fine needle into the baby's cord to replace some of his blood with blood that was cross-matched with Olivia's. If the cord became bruised, or they damaged a blood vessel, her baby could die during the procedure.

'I'd be with you tomorrow if I could,' Kelly had said. 'But there's no one else to cover the ER with Jake being off on vacation.' Jake was Kelly's colleague who worked the opposite shifts.

'That's okay,' Olivia had said.

'But you really shouldn't be on your own, girl. There must be someone. What about one of the nurses from the ER? You're friendly with most of them, aren't you? I could ask one of them. I think Patsy is off tomorrow.'

It was typical of Kelly. She loved to run the ER staff's lives in and out of the department. Left to her own devices, Olivia had no doubt that Kelly would frogmarch Patsy or one of the others upstairs.

'I won't be alone,' Olivia said. It was the only way to get Kelly off her case. 'Dr Stuart said he'd stay with me. He has a day off tomorrow.'

Kelly raised an eyebrow, but to Olivia's relief said nothing.

'I'd be grateful if you kept that fact to yourself.'

Kelly pretended to look offended. 'Me? You're asking me to keep my mouth shut? Do you have any idea how difficult that is when you have a juicy piece of gossip?' Her dark brown eyes softened. 'Don't worry, girl, you have enough on your plate without rumours spreading across the hospital about you and the gorgeous Dr Stuart.'

Kelly had stayed a little longer before kissing Olivia

on the cheek and telling her that she'd look in the next day to see how the procedure had gone. In a short while it would all be over.

The door swung open and David appeared, holding a bunch of mixed wild flowers. Looking sheepish, he placed them on the bedside table.

'Sorry, I would have been here earlier but I had to take Bouncer to doggy day care. He was a bit reluctant to go. I think he's pining for you.'

'Bouncer always did have a sixth sense as far as I'm concerned,' Olivia responded. They had given her something to sedate her just before David had come in and she was beginning to feel very sleepy—as if everything that was happening to her was happening to someone else.

'You'll stay with me?' she asked, reaching for David's hand. 'I'm scared. So very, very scared.'

'I'll stay,' David said quietly, and he bent and brushed her mouth with his lips. 'For as long as you need me.'

They came for her a few moments later and took her down to Theatre. She was vaguely aware of a lot of activity going on around her, and she desperately wanted to keep her eyes open so she could know how her baby reacted to the transfusion. But she felt so damned tired.

When she opened her eyes, it was all over. Dr Washington was looking down at her and if someone could frown and smile at the same time, that's what he was doing. Instantly alarmed, she struggled to sit up, but David pushed her gently back down on the pillow.

'It's good news.' Dr Washington got straight to the point. 'Your baby has responded well to the transfusion.'

Olivia's eyes sought David's. When he nodded she let out a whoosh of relief. But something was still wrong— she could tell.

'Now, Olivia, we've confirmed that your baby was very anaemic and we took some fetal blood to test for possible reasons. The results showed two things.' Dr Washington appeared to be choosing his words with care. 'First, your baby's blood cells are covered in antibodies. That means your antibodies have been crossing the placental barrier into his bloodstream. The second thing we know for certain is that your blood group is O positive. Correct?'

Olivia nodded.

'And your late husband was O positive too?'

'Yes.' Olivia's skin instantly chilled and nausea pooled in her belly. She reached for David's hand and felt a little better when his fingers squeezed hers.

'And your pregnancy is a result of IVF?'

Olivia nodded again. 'As I explained. My husband and I had an unsuccessful attempt at IVF while he was in remission. The remaining embryos were frozen. This pregnancy is from one of those embryos. Our embryos.'

'Then I don't know what to tell you. Your baby is Kell positive, which as you know is impossible unless your husband's results were wrong. And...' Dr Washington paused. 'That would have been the most likely scenario, but there's something else. This is going to be a shock. Your baby's blood group is AB.'

There was a heavy silence in the room as Olivia tried to take in what she was being told.

If the baby's blood group was AB then the baby couldn't be hers *or* Richard's. Which was impossible. She felt so groggy it was difficult to think clearly.

There were only two possibilities. Either the lab had made a mistake and got her baby's blood samples mixed up or—her head refused to go down that route.

'I'm sorry, Olivia. There's no mistake. The baby you are carrying is not yours or Richard's.'

Olivia swallowed hard. Then, before she knew it, she was sobbing and David was holding her in his arms.

For a second, David considered hightailing it out of the room. How the hell had he managed to get himself embroiled in this situation?

Before he'd met Olivia his life had been just fine. He'd had his work, a woman on his arm and in his bed whenever it had suited him, and as much time to himself as he'd wanted. The only blot in an otherwise perfect life had been finding himself sleeping on his friend Simon's couch—or rather not sleeping—and that was temporary and fixable.

But he couldn't leave her now. What sort of chicken-livered man would he be to walk out on a woman—a colleague—in distress? But this damsel was in a whole lot of trouble. Pregnant with her dead husband's child—or rather pregnant, but *not* with her and her dead husband's child, but a baby that essentially belonged to someone else, and who had a pretty grim prognosis. If he could have listed all the factors that would have made him steer clear of this woman, she would have ticked every box.

Olivia had stopped crying and pushed him away. She sniffed loudly and blew her nose. The way she was biting her lip, the way she was regarding the obs man with steel in her eyes, made him want to cheer. She had received a devastating blow, but she was dealing with it. He could only watch in admiration.

'What now?' Olivia asked quietly.

'We will transfuse the baby again in a couple of weeks.' Dr Washington wiped his brow. 'There is another complication. As you are not the biological mother of this child, or your late husband the biological father, we have a duty to try and contact whoever is and let them know we need to do a transfusion.'

Olivia closed her eyes. When she opened them again, her expression was resolute.

'In that case, we need to find out who it is, and quickly.'

Olivia was packing her things when David strode into the room.

'Are you ready?' he asked. 'If you are, your steed awaits.'

'I can easily take a cab,' Olivia protested.

David shook his head. 'Absolutely not.' He picked up her bag. 'Ready?'

Olivia hadn't the energy to argue. Besides, it was good to have someone take charge. She was physically and mentally exhausted. But she had crossed one hurdle. Her baby was fine—for now.

'Thank you,' she said simply.

She was grateful that he didn't say anything during the half-hour drive. She needed time to think things through. During the journey her thoughts kept flying from one incredible fact to another.

When they unlocked the door to Olivia's home, Bouncer charged over to her and covered her face with licks before leaping up on David and giving him the same treatment.

'You don't have to stay,' Olivia told David. 'In fact, I'd rather be on my own.'

David looked uncertain. 'If you're sure?'

'Absolutely.' Her voice wobbled and she blinked rapidly, swallowing hard on the lump that had risen to her throat. She wasn't at all sure. She was barely holding it together.

Something flickered in his eyes. 'Sit down,' he ordered. He took a throw from the back of the couch and placed it over her knees. All Olivia could think of was that she had to look like his gran now—as if looking mumsy hadn't been bad enough.

'I'll be back in a sec,' David said. He coaxed Bouncer into the kitchen and closed the door. Then he came to sit next to Olivia.

'Let's look at this logically,' he said.

Logically? How the hell was she supposed to do that? But he was right. She had to think. Think clearly. Now was not the time to fall apart.

'You've passed the first hurdle. The transfusion went well and your baby is in no immediate danger. Now, what about the fact that the baby is not your biological child? Any idea how that could have happened?'

Olivia drew in a sharp intake of breath. 'The clinic must have got my embryos mixed up with somebody else's. Either when they were doing the embryo transfer, or at some point after fertilisation. But how?' She shook her head. 'I can't imagine.'

'You should make an appointment to see the director at the IVF clinic as soon as possible. Do you have the number? I'll call them and set it up.'

She nodded and scrambled around in her bag for her diary. She opened it at the correct page and handed it to David. Having something concrete to do made her feel better.

Something else hit her. If the wrong embryos had been implanted into her, then the embryos that had come from her and Richard must have been implanted into someone else.

'But if it's not my baby, whose is it?' She gulped. 'I mean…' she stood up and started pacing 'If I had the wrong embryo implanted, then someone must have mine. Perhaps from three years ago. …does that mean there might be a child belonging to Richard and me out there somewhere? Oh, God, what a mess.' She thought she was going to lose it again.

David walked over to her and gripped her by the shoulders. 'Hey, close your eyes and breathe,' he said.

He sat down next to her and she swayed into him. His arms tightened around her and she felt herself relax.

He waited until she had her breathing under control. 'Hang on in there, Olivia. Everything's going to be okay. I'm going to help you. Do you understand?'

His voice was low, but he spoke with such conviction she believed him. She had to believe him. When she opened her eyes he tilted her chin with his finger. 'You're tough, Olivia—we both know that. But you—we—have to deal with one thing at a time. Okay?'

She nodded.

'First, let me set up a meeting with the clinic. The sooner you have those answers, the better.'

He took his phone from his pocket and moved away. Olivia was only vaguely conscious of him saying very firmly that Olivia needed to see the director of the clinic as soon as possible. Today. No, tomorrow wouldn't do.

'They can see you as soon as you can make it down there,' he said. 'I'll drive you, of course.'

It was a relief to have David take over. Her head was still buzzing with the ramifications of the baby not being hers.

'You need a lawyer, so do you have a preference? I can contact my family's firm if you like. They'll put us in touch with someone in San Francisco who might have experience in this sort of thing.'

'This sort of thing? Lawyers? Oh, God.'

David took her hands in his. 'You have to think about hiring an attorney, Olivia.'

'I can't. Not right now…perhaps later. After we've seen the people at the clinic. It still might be a horrible mistake.' But even without seeing the expression on David's face she knew that the only mistake was the one the clinic must have made.

'Can I call someone for you? A friend? Your father?'

'My best friend is living in the UK. She's thirty-six weeks pregnant herself and they'll never allow her to fly—even if I wanted her to. And as for Dad, I'll talk to him when I know more. He'll only get really anxious and insist on flying out here. When I know exactly what I'm dealing with I'll talk to them both.'

'Are you feeling well enough to go to the clinic? I could insist that they come here.'

'That might take longer to organise. No, let's just get this over with.'

David steered the car through the streets of the city, wondering for the umpteenth time how on earth he'd managed to get himself caught up so completely in someone else's life. It wasn't that he didn't sympathise with Olivia—it was an unbelievably awful situation, but he'd spent the best part of his adult life avoiding emotional involvement, and yet somehow here he was, up to his neck in someone else's.

He'd wanted to leave when he'd taken her home. Every nerve in his body had screamed at him to get the hell out of there—colleague or not, in trouble or not. Olivia wasn't his problem after all. But one look at her pale face, the stubborn lift of her chin, the faint tremor of her lips that she'd tried so hard to hide, and he'd just been unable to do it. So he'd take her to her appointment, go in with her if she wished, but then he'd drop her home and that would be that. She must have other people who would be better at offering support than he was—her father for example. So before he left he'd persuade her to call him. He sneaked a look at the woman sitting next to him. She was still pale but looked composed, and there was a determined set to her mouth, as if she was preparing to do battle.

He'd said she was tough and she was. She'd be fine without him. She had to be.

CHAPTER TEN

OLIVIA studied Dr Fulton in disbelief. Next to the dark-haired gynaecologist was a man in a grey suit with short hair and a bland expression. He was the clinic's attorney, Mr Crighton. Beside him was another man, roughly the same age as the lawyer, whom Dr Fulton had introduced as the new clinical director, Dr Lovatt.

David had offered to come in with her and she'd agreed. She knew only too well that when faced with bad news, patients took in little of what was being said and often needed the person who had been with them to remember the details of the conversation. She couldn't afford to miss one word.

'I'm so sorry, Dr Simpson. What can I say?' Dr Lovatt said. 'As soon as we received your phone call we went over every step of your treatment and our records show that there was a couple who were in the same day you were. We managed to narrow down the possibilities to a woman who had her eggs retrieved immediately after you did. As you will be aware, we remove the eggs and fertilise them with the partner's sperm straight after collection. This is indeed what happened with you and the other couple. However, for some reason we can't yet explain but will probably have to put down to human error, it seems that our embryologist labelled the dishes containing yours and this other couple's embryos incorrectly. The embryologist doesn't work for us any longer, if that's any consolation.'

It was as Olivia had expected, but nevertheless she wasn't prepared for the way her heart dropped to her shoes. Part of her, she knew, had still been hoping that it was the hospital that had got everything mixed up.

'Not really,' Olivia said. 'There's no point in going over what happened. What I need to know is what happens next.'

'We are in the process of contacting the biological father and apprising him of the situation. We have to wait for him to make a decision.'

'By a decision, what do you mean exactly?'

Dr Fulton twiddled with her glasses, clearly uncomfortable. She glanced at the attorney.

'It's not clear at this stage who has legal parentage of the baby you are carrying,' Mr Crighton said flatly.

Olivia's heart thumped against her ribs. 'You can't mean that he could take the baby from me?'

'I'm sorry. There have been cases like this before, unfortunately, that have gone to court. There is no hard and fast rule as to who gets custody—it can go either way in these cases,' Crighton continued.

Olivia felt sick. She hadn't even considered that they might try to take her baby. 'I'd rather you didn't talk about me and my child as a case,' she said frostily. She leaned over the desk. 'Let me tell you. I will fight tooth and nail to keep *my* son. You said biological father. What about his wife? What does she have to say?'

Dr Fulton pressed her lips together. 'I am sorry, but I can't divulge any more information about the couple's circumstances at this point. All communication is likely to be through his attorney.' She folded her hands. 'We will, of course, compensate you.'

'Compensate me! You think any amount of money is going to compensate me for the loss of my baby?' She was so angry she could hardly speak. She stood up and placed her hands on the desk. 'Because, believe me, this is my baby.'

Dr Fulton blanched. 'I suggest you think about hiring an attorney too.'

So it had come to this.

'Dr Simpson intends to contact an attorney as soon as she leaves here.' This came from David, who up until now had been sitting quietly and listening intently.

'Where are my embryos?' She had to know. 'Do I have a child out there?'

Dr Fulton shook her head. 'No, I'm sorry. The pregnancies using your embryos did not continue. I am so very sorry.'

It was another blow—but in a way it made it easier. She didn't know if she could have coped with the fact that she might have a child out there, being brought up by another couple.

'So this couple—the ones who are the biological parents of the baby I'm carrying—' she couldn't keep referring to her baby as an embryo '—have no children?' Despite everything, Olivia's heart went out to them. She had firsthand experience of failed IVF, and knew how devastating it was. 'I'm sorry.'

'I understand that the baby you are carrying has fetal anaemia,' Crighton said, after a pause. 'We have to inform the biological father of anything that involves the health of his child.'

'Why?'

'It is normal procedure.'

'He can't try to prevent me from going ahead with any treatment that my child needs!' Olivia's head was throbbing. She removed her hands from the desk. 'I will fight him every inch of the way. But right now it seems I have to inform him that my baby will need another blood transfusion in order to save his life.' To her horror her voice cracked. She took a deep breath. She had to hold it together. Her baby depended on it. 'Make no mistake. *My son*—' she emphasised the last two words '—is going to have that transfusion. I don't give a pig's ear what the so-called genetic father has to say about it. He can sue me for every cent I have if he likes.'

David reached out and took her hand. 'Listen to me, Olivia. I don't imagine he'll withhold consent. If he wants the baby, he's hardly likely to want to put his health in jeopardy. From what Dr Fulton is saying, he will have only just found out about the situation. He and his wife will need time to decide what to do. In the meantime, all you can do is hire your own attorney and do everything you can to make sure you deliver a healthy baby.'

David was right. Until she knew her baby was going to be okay, it was all that she could deal with.

'Tell him that I would be grateful for his speedy response. Tell him…' She hesitated. 'Tell him that I have no intention of giving up my baby. Tell him that the decent thing to do—the only thing to do—is to leave me and my child in peace.' A thought struck her. She'd been so caught up in what was happening she hadn't thought about it before. 'If our embryos did get mixed up, I had another four still in storage.' The throbbing in her temples was getting worse. 'Can you at least tell me what has happened to them? It doesn't make any difference to the fact that I am going to fight to keep this baby, but I would like to know.'

Dr Fulton looked away. 'I'm sorry, I can't tell you that, but...' She reached out to take Olivia's hand. 'Please don't count on it.'

Olivia's knees were weak as she walked out the door. As he followed her out of the room, David said something to the doctors and the attorney that she couldn't hear.

She took a deep breath and clasped her hands together. 'Thank you for coming in with me, David.' She tried a smile. 'I bet you didn't expect all this when you offered to house-sit for me.'

'I think you should call your father. Or is there anyone else nearer?' He took her hands in his and she felt his strength flow into her.

'No. But, look, you must have things to do. I'll be okay from here. Honestly.'

David looked at her for a long moment. 'There's nothing important I have to do right now. At the very least let me run you home.'

The truth was she couldn't bear to be alone with her thoughts. 'Thank you,' she said simply.

When they arrived at her house, David came around to her door and held out a hand. She waved him away. She simply wasn't going to behave like an invalid. He watched her with amusement in his intense blue eyes as Olivia wriggled out of the low-slung sports car, her bump making the manoeuvre an awkward and ungainly feat that required her total concentration.

'Really, David, there's no need for you to stay. I'll manage perfectly from here.'

'And who is going to walk that steamroller on legs

you have inside there? I think I should stay. For a couple of nights at any rate.'

He had a point. Bouncer would have her over on her feet, especially now that her balance wasn't what it used to be. Nevertheless, the thought of having David living in her house when she felt so vulnerable and emotional was more than she could cope with.

But he didn't give her a chance to protest further. He was carrying her bag into the hallway, and she was being led into her sitting room and made to sit on her couch. Then her legs were being lifted, a pillow placed behind her back and a rug thrown over her knees. Bouncer, sensing something was wrong, settled himself quietly alongside her, placing his soft head on her chest. She had to laugh.

She pushed the blanket away and sat up. 'This isn't going to help. I'm not ill, and I need to work out what to do next. I can't just sit here and do nothing.'

David pressed her back down. 'Yes, you can. For a while. You've been through a lot in the last forty-eight hours. Think of what you would say to a patient.'

He was right. She was so tired all of a sudden. So very tired. She would just close her eyes for a moment. Then she would decide what to do.

When she opened her eyes the sky was turning from black to light blue, and Bouncer was snoring softly beside her. On the chair opposite, David was asleep, his long legs stretched out in front of him.

Despite everything, she'd slept. And slept soundly.

She threw the blankets off and shoved Bouncer onto the floor. He gave her an offended look before padding towards the kitchen. Taking one of the blankets from the couch, she very gently covered David. He was frowning in his sleep, as if whatever he was dreaming about troubled him.

As she stood looking down at him, her heart contracted. She knew he would rather be anywhere else but here, but he'd stayed. He was a better man than he thought he was. One day he would fall in love and make some woman very happy. Her heart ached at the thought.

Quietly, so as not to disturb him, she tiptoed into the kitchen and set about feeding Bouncer. Before she showered she'd take him down to the small beach that was only a short walk away.

She brushed her hair and changed quickly before quietly letting herself and Bouncer out. She knew the path so well she could have found her way in almost complete darkness. She hurried down towards the shore, enjoying the early morning breeze on her face. The end of the path opened up onto the beach and as the sun started to rise, it turned the sea aquamarine and Olivia caught her breath. How could she lose her baby when the world was such a beautiful place? She found a flat rock to sit on while Bouncer ran around, barking with delight.

She heard the crunch of sand, and as Bouncer flew past her, his tail wagging furiously, she didn't have to look behind her to know that it was David.

He sat down next to her and put his arm around her shoulder. As if it were the most natural thing in the world she leaned into him, inhaling the musky scent of his skin, feeling his strong arm holding her tight. She felt possessed by a strange calm.

She would not lose her baby. She simply would not allow it to happen. And her baby was going to be just fine. He would come through the second transfusion as easily as he'd come through the first. He'd be delivered at thirty-four weeks and he'd be okay. He would be looked after by the best doctors in one of the best and most up-to-date hospitals in the world. She had to keep believing that.

'How did you know where to look for me?' she asked after a while.

She heard the smile in David's voice. 'Simply listened for the sound of Bouncer's bark. Are you all right?'

She pushed her face against his chest. It felt good to be held. So good. Then the tears came and she couldn't stop them. She wasn't just crying, she was howling—a horrified, separate part of her noticed—howling like a baby, and David was holding her, just holding her while she let it all out.

Eventually the tears stopped and she disentangled herself from his arms. He held out his handkerchief and she blew her nose loudly. She could barely look at him, she felt so embarrassed. What must he be thinking? Somehow he'd become immersed in her problems and they were nothing to do with him. Of all the people she could have picked—not that she'd even picked him— he was the most unlikely candidate to support a woman who was in emotional shreds.

'I'm sorry,' she sniffed when she managed to speak again. 'You try to help a colleague in trouble and you end up watching her go through meltdown.' She straightened her shoulders. 'Look, David, you've been great, but you don't have to keep doing this, you know. I'm not your responsibility. I feel bad enough without worrying that I've dragged you in to my problems.'

'Hey,' David said softly. 'I've never had to think of anyone besides myself. It feels good.' He bent down and kissed the tip of her nose. 'I think you're good for my soul.'

* * *

David was torn. Despite what he'd told Olivia, he did have reservations. Crying women were not his forte. He'd seen women cry, of course, sometimes when he was ending the relationship, and the first sign of a tear trembling on an eyelash was usually enough to send him sprinting in the opposite direction. And he'd never seen anyone cry like this, as if they were being torn from the inside. Not even his mother, after Lisa's accident. No wonder he didn't want to get involved with a woman— apart from his mother, they were so emotional.

On the other hand, he'd always had a thing for wounded birds and a man didn't walk away from something just because he didn't have the stomach for it. He certainly didn't walk away from a woman in trouble— no matter how much he wanted to.

And that was the other odd thing. He didn't really want to. Over these last few weeks he'd come to realise that out of all the women he'd ever known, Olivia was the one he felt most comfortable with. He'd never been happier than when they'd been sitting side by side, him with a beer in one hand, her with her ridiculous herbal tea, watching the game on TV. That she was beautiful he'd always known—he remembered only too well his instant reaction to her when he'd first clapped eyes on her—but she also made him laugh. He felt good when he was with her.

She was a friend—just a friend. Although he had to keep reminding himself of that.

He'd never had a woman friend before, and it was an entirely novel situation. His male friends never talked about anything except work, how their favourite team was doing, or where they'd been over the weekend. They rarely discussed girlfriends or wives, and never, ever, personal problems. That's precisely what he liked about being with his male friends.

And if this particular friend had a shed-load of problems, that too would pass. Then he could get on with his life.

Later, after they'd had breakfast and showered, David suggested they go for a drive.

'It'll do you good to get out for a while, and I have just the place in mind.'

He looked so pleased with his suggestion she hadn't the heart to refuse.

The sun was high in the sky as they headed out of town, and Olivia felt herself relax. For the rest of today, even just for a few hours, she wasn't going to dwell on what might or might not happen. It was out of her control now.

The sun bounced off the sea, shooting sparks towards the sky. How could anyone think that the future was anything but bright on a day like this?

'There is a restaurant someone told me about, a couple of hours' drive away. He says you can see the ocean and watch eagles flying past while you eat.'

'Sounds good to me,' Olivia said, clutching onto her seat as David took one of the hairpin bends too fast for her liking. 'Hey, slow down,' she said. 'We've got some precious cargo in the car.'

To her relief, David immediately brought the car down to a more sedate fifty. 'Sorry, I keep forgetting.'

Something in his expression made her pause. Was it regret?

'Anyway, the point is to admire the scenery. We can't do that while I'm watching where you're driving.'

David grinned at her. 'Trust me, you don't have to watch where I'm going. I know exactly where I'm going.'

Was there hidden meaning in the words? David did seem to be focussed on one thing in his life—his job. But apart from that? Did he think about the future at all?

'One day I'll be chief of surgery at one of the New York hospitals,' he said, as if he'd read her mind.

The thought of David not being in her life dismayed her. 'How can you think of going back to New York when you have all this on your doorstep?'

He sent her another grin. 'Pace of life is too slow here for me.' His lips twitched. 'Having said that, life hasn't exactly been boring lately.'

So that was all she was to him? A diversion? A bit of excitement? No, she couldn't believe that. David might not see her as anything but a friend and colleague, but he had to care about her—even just a little. Or was he just hanging around out of some kind of old-fashioned sense of chivalry? After all, everything she knew about him pointed in that direction.

She pushed the gloomy thought away. Hadn't she just told herself she was going to enjoy the day and think only good, happy thoughts? It had been a long time since she'd driven down the Pacific Highway. The coastal road was breathtaking—in more ways than one.

Suddenly David pulled into a car park. 'There's something I want you to see,' he said mysteriously.

Olivia followed him out and down a path through some cedar trees. Suddenly the view opened up and the Pacific Ocean stretched before them. There was also a strong smell of fish and what only could be described as honking noises.

'Look,' David pointed to the beach below. 'I was driving this way the other day and came across them.'

A pack of enormous seals was sunning on the rocks. 'Elephant seals,' David said, watching her face closely. 'Aren't they the weirdest things you've ever seen?'

'And the smelliest!' But she smiled. She had the distinct impression David was going out of his way to distract her. She'd been here before, years ago, before Richard had got ill. But David looked so pleased with his impromptu detour that she couldn't bring herself to tell him. Something glowed inside her. David had to care about her. Or else he was very good at pretending.

When they were back on their way again, David slid a look at Olivia. She had a small smile playing on her lips. The side visit to the seals had worked a treat.

He made sure he was driving at a safe pace. When she'd asked him if he'd forgotten she was pregnant, it had come as a surprise. The truth was that he had. Just for a few minutes he'd allowed himself to forget that Olivia was carrying another man's child and that one day soon he'd be out of her life and she out of his. He should have felt relief, but to his surprise he felt anything but that.

'How did you find this place?' Olivia asked when they went into the restaurant. It was built into the cliff and had dramatic views of the sea and the coastline below. 'I've been living in San Francisco for years and never knew it existed.'

David looked smug as they were shown to their table at the window. 'One of the benefits of being new to a city is that people are always telling you about their favourite places.'

Olivia tried to ignore the feeling of relief that swept through her. She would have hated to think that this was somewhere David frequented with his girlfriends. She had to stop thinking about that. However, not thinking about David and not thinking about her baby left very little to think about.

'How's your friend's baby?' she asked. 'Has she stopped crying?'

'Not sure. Since I moved into my apartment I hardly see them. The last time I was at their place, though, she did seem happier. Either I've become immune or she cries less.'

He stretched his long legs in front of him and somehow, she wasn't sure how, they became entangled with hers. For a heart-stopping moment she couldn't move. Then, trying not to make a big thing of it, she moved hers away. There was no way she could think straight with his legs touching hers.

Despite her attempts to be subtle, he must have noticed. He raised an eyebrow and grinned and colour surged to her cheeks.

'Is it just you and your sister? What about your parents? You haven't mentioned them.' Actually, he'd made it clear that he didn't want to talk about his family. She was babbling in an attempt to cover her embarrassment.

'God, no. There are four of us. Two girls, me and my brother.'

'It must have been fun growing up with siblings.'

'It was—for a while.'

'And your mother? What's she like?'

'Elegant and cold. We never had that much to do with her—or my father.' His expression darkened. 'We were raised by a string of nannies. As soon as we were old enough we were sent away to school.'

Olivia was shocked. In her mind mothers were loving, caring, warm people who wanted to spend as much time with their children as possible.

'Were you very well off?' She knew he was, but of

course she couldn't say that. 'I mean, I assume only the wealthy have nannies.'

'You could say that—at least, my father is.'

Getting him to talk was like drawing blood from a stone.

'What does that mean?'

'It means that my father is very wealthy. He and my mother are separated but he's always been generous with his money. At least as long as you do what he wants.' He regarded her steadily. 'To be honest, my father and I aren't on speaking terms. And as for my mother, elder sister and my brother, I don't have much to do with them either.'

'Why is that?' She couldn't imagine not speaking to her father.

'Look, can we leave it?' David said. 'Just take it that I don't do the whole family thing, and as I have no intention of getting married, it hardly matters.'

'Why are you so against marriage?' she persisted. She wanted to understand what made him tick.

'I'm not against it. I think it's great—for other people.'

A large bird flew past almost at eye level and Olivia smiled with delight.

David turned to see what she was looking at. When he saw the bird swooping down the cliff, his expression turned even darker. 'See that bird?' he said. 'That's the only way to be. Free and unencumbered.' He picked up his menu, the expression on his face making it clear that the subject was closed. 'Now, shall we order?'

Seeing that it appeared every other topic was out of bounds, the rest of their meal was spent talking about medicine. After lunch they drove back but, unlike the journey out, they were both preoccupied with their own thoughts.

When they reached her house she was horrified to find her driveway filled with paparazzi.

As they drove up to the door, flash bulbs popped and reporters tried to push microphones in her face.

'Dr Simpson, can you tell us how you feel?'

'Dr Simpson, is it true that you are carrying a baby that belongs to someone else?'

'Dr Simpson, can you tell us what you are going to do? Will you fight to keep the baby?'

Olivia was aghast. How had they found out? She glanced at David whose mouth was set in a grim line. 'I could take you to a hotel,' he said.

'No. I'm not going to let then hound me out of my home.'

David pulled up in front of her door. 'Go inside,' he said. 'I'll deal with them.'

'Could you?' she said. Although she hated that David was being dragged into her mess, she didn't have the strength to deal with the reporters. Not right now. Anyway, what right did anyone have to know about her life?

David leaped out of the car and stood in front of the door, shielding her as she let herself in.

'Dr Simpson is not taking or answering questions at this moment,' he said, but with a smile that reminded Olivia of a wolf. 'I suggest that you leave your cards and as soon as she has a statement we will get in touch with you.'

'Dr Stuart, David, are you involved with Dr Simpson?'

This time there was amusement in David's voice. 'Dr Simpson and I are colleagues and friends. No more. Now, as I said, I suggest you leave your cards and we will contact you if and when we have something to say.'

Clearly the reporters weren't happy with his response,

as they continued asking their questions, but David simply closed the door in their faces. He did it gently and politely but firmly.

'How did they find out?' Olivia asked. 'The clinic has to keep the information confidential.'

The polite smile David had plastered to his face disappeared and he was frowning. 'They might have found out about you because of me,' he said eventually.

'You mean because you've been in the papers? Because of your sister?'

'Exactly.' He rubbed his chin, his stubble rasping under his fingers. 'I'm sorry. If that is the case I've made matters worse for you instead of better. It never occurred to me that they would track me down here.'

'It's not your fault,' Olivia said tiredly. 'Besides, you can't be sure it was you. Look, thanks for looking after Bouncer for me, and thanks for the day out, but really I'll be fine from here.'

David shook his head. 'I'm staying,' he said firmly. 'I can't leave you here with those vultures outside, particularly as I might have brought them here in the first place. I have the weekend off. Think of it as having your own personal butler for the next few days.'

The atmosphere between them was strained and, uncertain how to heal the rift that seemed to have opened up between them, Olivia told David that she was going to bed as soon as she'd walked Bouncer. David offered to take Bouncer himself, saying he needed a run, and seeing Olivia had no desire to face the reporters again, she gave in without protest.

When she woke the next morning, she padded towards the kitchen to make herself a cup of tea. On the way she passed the door of the study. David was leaning back in the chair, studying the computer screen thoughtfully.

He must have heard her as he minimised the screen and whirled around.

'Hey. How are you today?' He smiled, back to his usual cheerful self.

'What were you looking at?'

'Nothing.' He jumped to his feet, looking guilty. 'Are you hungry? I could nip out and get us some pastries if you like?'

'I want to see what you were looking at.'

David sighed and sat back down. 'I'm not sure that you do want to.' Nevertheless, he brought the page he'd been studying back up. 'I thought I would do some research while you were still asleep. Now that your story is in the news, it has to be gloves off. The biological father will learn everything about you. It's only sensible to find out everything we can about him as well as research similar—er—cases.'

Olivia leaned over his shoulder. He was looking at a site about IVF errors. The blood in her veins turned to ice. There was no clear information as to who would gain custody, which meant there was a very real possibility she could lose her baby. The room spun and she had to grab onto the back of David's chair to keep on her feet.

David was out of his chair and had picked her up before her legs gave way. He carried her over to the sofa.

'It's not as bleak as it looks,' he murmured against her hair, before laying her down on the couch.

'It looks pretty bleak to me.'

David hesitated. 'I know you didn't want me to look into the couple...' he shrugged '...but I thought I would anyway.'

For the first time since she'd found herself in this

horrible mess, anger flashed through her. 'You had no right. This is my life.'

David regarded her steadily. 'I know how you feel, believe me. But as a doctor, before you do anything you try to find out as much as possible, don't you?'

She nodded.

'So why should this be any different?'

'It just is. I took your advice and put this in the hands of my attorney. Shouldn't we leave it to her? My God, David, if you give the courts any reason to decide against me…'

He sat down next to her and took her hand. 'Sweetie. You have one chance at this. If they take the baby from you at birth and give him to the biological parents, it is even more unlikely you'll ever get him back. Is that a risk you want to take?'

The thought of her baby being taken from her, even for a few days, was unbearable. Besides, she couldn't not ask what David had found out. Any damage to her case would have already been done.

'Go on, then, tell me.'

'Okay. The father is a doctor, an orthopod. He's the one that is bringing the case.'

'On his own?'

'It seems he and his wife are no longer together. They divorced a couple of years ago.'

Olivia felt the first stirring of optimism. She'd worried that her single mother status would count against her, but if the father was single too, at least that put them on an equal footing.

'Doesn't his ex-wife have a say?'

'Now, here's the thing. She couldn't produce her own eggs so they used a donor. One of those college girls who donate eggs as a way of funding their degree.'

'How do you know all this?'

David stood. 'I think there's something you should see.' He crossed over to her, a newspaper in his hand. 'One of the reporters left this on the front step. It's this morning's edition of *The Gazette*.'

Olivia pushed the hair from her face. The photograph was on the front page and the caption read '*Doc involved in IVF mix-up moves his egg donor in*'.

Bemused, she studied the photograph. It was of a young woman standing in the door in her nightdress, with a cast on her right leg. Her eyes were wide and her expression shocked. Clearly she hadn't expected to find journalists on the doorstep.

Then she read the story. It explained that Lily Greyson, age twenty-seven, had been identified as the egg donor in the '*Baby Mix-up Scandal*'.

She read it through once, then again. Apparently Lily had donated her eggs to the clinic five years ago as a way of financing her studies. She was a nurse at one of the San Francisco hospitals. Despite everything, that bit made Olivia smile. Her baby might not be hers biologically but it seemed she and the biological parents had something else in common apart from the baby—a love of medicine.

She tried to take it all in. She'd heard of sites that offered donor eggs, usually from Ivy League graduates, but surely that was anonymous? Nevertheless, it had to help her case.

Now she knew about Lily, she understood why the clinic had only ever mentioned the father. For the first time since she'd learned about the mistake her spirits lifted. If this woman was the donor and had freely given away her eggs, surely she would have few rights when it came to making a claim? There was also the added relief of not having to compete with the biological mother when it came to custody of her child. It was something that had lain heavily on her mind. Although she had no intention of giving up her baby, the thought of what losing the child would mean for the biological mother was one of the things that had worried her most. Now she no longer had to worry that she was fighting a woman who wanted the baby as much as she did.

'So that's why they keep talking about the father and not the mother,' she said to David.

'I think there's a good chance this will help swing things your way,' he replied. She smiled up at him and their eyes locked. Olivia was acutely aware of her pulse racing.

There was a breathless silence between them, and it was David who looked away first. 'The biological mother's rights are tenuous at best,' he continued. 'She signed her rights away when she made the donation. And the ex-wife doesn't appear to have any interest in making a claim either. In fact...' he sucked in a breath '...there's something else I've found out. I'm sorry to tell you, but as a couple they had the remainder of their embryos destroyed.'

Olivia shuddered. She knew what that meant. Any hope of her having another baby with her and Richard's embryos was gone. But that no longer mattered so much. What really mattered was keeping the baby she was carrying, who might not be genetically hers or Richard's but who she couldn't love any more even if he had been.

'So let me get this right. The father wants custody of my baby, even though he destroyed the embryos he thought were his? He's no longer married and the donor has no claim?' Surely her claim had to be stronger?

She sighed. She hated thinking about her baby in those terms.

'That is more or less the way it appears to me.'

'What is he like—the father?' Olivia wasn't at all sure if she wanted to know. She didn't want to think of him as a person.

David shrugged. 'All I know is that he's an orthopaedic attending in a San Francisco hospital. In the meantime, I think you should let your lawyer know everything, in case she hasn't heard already.'

'I'll do that now, 'Olivia replied, getting to her feet.

'I'm going to go and fetch some clothes,' David said. 'I'll stock up with provisions while I'm at it.'

'Don't you have plans to go back to New York this weekend?' Olivia asked. She couldn't imagine what his girlfriend would think when she saw the papers. But no doubt David would explain.

'I rescheduled for next weekend while you were sleeping,' he said. He'd never said anything about who he was seeing, and Olivia wasn't sure she wanted to know. On the other hand, if David's involvement with *her* was making things complicated for him, perhaps she should talk to his girlfriend?

'Is there anyone you'd like me to speak to and explain?' she asked.

He frowned and shook his head. 'Explain what? That I'm helping a friend out? Besides, I'll see Lisa next weekend.'

So there was a girlfriend. Of course there was. Despite everything, the thought made her heart sink.

CHAPTER ELEVEN

DAVID returned a couple of hours later. In the meantime, Olivia had spoken to her lawyer. She hadn't been reassured by the conversation.

'How are you doing?' David asked, giving her a keen look.

'I've been better.' Olivia gave a shaky laugh. 'It doesn't help that the reporters keep trying to look in the windows.'

'What did your attorney have to say?'

'A bunch of legalese. Basically that I will probably have to go to court and fight for the right to keep my baby. It seems that the biological father definitely intends to fight for custody.'

A muscle twitched in David's cheek.

'And the donor. Surely she must have a stake in all of this?'

'His side isn't really saying anything. All the communication is with the father only.' She sighed. 'If only I could go directly to the couple, talk to them, make them see how much this baby means to me. How much I want him.' Her voice broke and David scooped her into his arms.

'It's going to be all right, sweetheart, I promise you, I'm going to make sure that it is.'

* * *

Olivia was sure the weekend cooped up together was going to be awkward. After David had hugged her, they'd broken apart and started talking about trivia before making their excuses and going to their separate bedrooms. Come to think of it—where was he? Curled up on the couch with Bouncer beside her, she realised she hadn't seen or heard David since teatime. Olivia shrugged and turned her concentration back to her book. Probably on the phone to his girlfriend.

Except it seemed she was wrong as he popped his head round the door. 'Hey—can I show you something?'

Olivia frowned. 'What is it?'

'You'll see.' He tilted his head, eyes glinting, as he motioned her to follow. It seemed Bouncer didn't need encouragement as he bounded down onto the floor.

'Traitor,' Olivia grumbled underneath her breath at her dog. Curious, she followed David up the stairs and towards her room. Her heart thumped—surely he wasn't going to try to seduce her?

No more had the thought rattled round her head and sent a tiny but ever so real spark of excitement down her backbone than he stopped and turned to her. 'Close your eyes.'

She stared at him, confusion making her hesitate.

As if he'd read her mind, he grinned. 'Come on—don't you trust me by now? Now, close them.' She felt his hand on her arm, holding it gently but firmly, his fingers burning her skin, his breath warm on her neck. 'Tighter—I can see you peeping.'

Laughter bubbled in her throat. It was like being a kid again. 'They are closed. Now come on, what is it?' Without letting her go, he positioned himself behind her, both his hands on her arms as he gently guided her forward. If she leant back just a few millimetres she knew that her back would be pressed up against his rock-hard chest. The longing to do just that, to be held in his arms, was almost overwhelming.

'Okay.' David's voice cut through her thoughts. 'What do you think?'

Olivia could only stare round in astonishment. Words failed her as she looked around the room off her bedroom that she'd planned to have as a nursery.

'Oh, God, don't you like it?' She could hear the anxiety in David's voice. 'I'm sorry—I should have checked with you first but I wanted to surprise you. Give you a boost after all the rubbish you've been through recently.'

She swallowed hard, not trusting herself to speak without her voice breaking. She had planned to get the decorators in when her pregnancy was further along. She hadn't wanted to do it before as a small part of her hadn't wanted to tempt fate. But it had all gone wrong anyway.

Now, with the nursery all painted and decorated, David was telling her that he had no doubt she'd be bringing her baby home. He had done exactly the right thing.

'David, it's beautiful. Thank you.'

'Do you like the fairy-lights over there?' He pointed to the sash window. 'Or would they be better above the cot? And what about the pictures on that wall—should I have put them over by the bookshelf?'

Olivia shook her head. 'No, you've done everything perfectly. It's exactly how I wanted it to look.' Her voice caught. 'Richard and I made a start on painting before he was too ill to do much else and I've been meaning to get round to doing the rest. Oh, my goodness! You've even put the cot together! Dad was meant to come out some weekend and help me with that, but what with everything going on I never got round to asking him again.'

She walked over and fingered the tiny duvet cover dotted with butterflies. Except something wasn't quite right... A smile tugged at the corner of her mouth as she looked over at him. 'I think the headboard's back to front.'

David frowned and studied his recent handiwork. He rubbed his chin with his hand. 'Mmm, I see what you mean. The painted side is meant to be facing the other way, isn't it?'

Olivia laughed. 'Let me guess—you didn't bother reading the instructions?'

He grinned back at her. 'Don't talk crazy, woman—I'm genetically programmed as a man not to read any instruction booklet under any circumstances.' He whipped out the screwdriver sticking out of his back pocket. 'But don't you worry, I'll have it sorted out in a blink of an eye.'

'Can I help?'

'No.' He pointed over to the rocking chair. 'You sit yourself down there and practise rocking.'

Instantly she bristled. 'Like an old woman, you mean?'

His eyes held hers. 'No.' He said, his voice low. 'Like the wonderful mother you're destined to be.'

Olivia stared back at him. 'You're really not the man you pretend to be, David Stuart,' she replied softly. Her heart jolted. No, he was the man she was falling in love with.

CHAPTER TWELVE

THE rest of the weekend passed all too quickly. David took Bouncer for his regular walks while Olivia huddled inside the house, out of sight of the cameras. They watched the San Francisco Giants games on TV, sitting side by side on the couch as if they were an ordinary couple instead of two friends under siege, Olivia with a mug of tea and David with coffee or a beer. At times she would catch David looking at her with a bemused expression on his face. On other occasions she would find herself watching him when she knew he couldn't see. There was something fizzing between them, that she was sure of, but it seemed as if neither of them wanted to explore just exactly what it was. Perhaps he simply felt sorry for her.

Whatever it was, she was grateful to him for his friendship, and relieved not to be going through this horrendous experience on her own.

On Monday, Olivia knew she had no option but to brave the cameras. She was due in at work, although in a couple of weeks she'd be starting her maternity leave. She dressed carefully, knowing that she looked awful. There were dark circles under her eyes, and her skin had an unhealthy pallor that no amount of foundation could disguise. She and David had discussed how they would deal with the press. He was also due back at work, and had offered to leave early, before it was light, so they could avoid being seen together, but Olivia had vetoed the plan. She was damned if she was going to let the media make her sneak around like a thief. It was her business and her business only.

But the barrage of flashing lights as she stepped out of the door made her panic. David took her by the elbow and steered her into his car.

'Dr Simpson, how are you holding up?' a reporter called out.

'Dr Simpson, will you give up your baby?'

'Olivia, look this way.'

She kept her head down and refused to answer their questions. By her side, David deflected their questions with a quip. Despite his light-hearted response to the press, she had never seen him look so angry.

When they were in the car he turned to her. 'Will you be okay for the rest of the week? On your own, I mean?'

'Yes, I'll be perfectly fine.' But she knew she'd miss him. Miss him terribly.

The staff stopped talking as she came into the ER room. There was no doubt who and what they'd been discussing moments earlier.

Kelly hurried forward and took her hands. 'Olivia, it's lovely to have you back.'

One by one the staff came up to her. Most hugged her, some just squeezed her shoulder, but every one of them made it clear by word or deed that they were on her side. Olivia had to hold back the tears. They'd always got along, but she'd had no idea of the depth of their feelings for her. Their support meant a lot.

'The press have been ringing the staff and asking questions,' Kelly said once she'd shooed everyone back to work. 'No one is saying anything. You can rely one hundred per cent on their discretion.'

She studied Olivia. 'But should you even be here? Forgive me, honey, but you look like hell.'

'Kelly, when are you going to say something nice to me?'

'Are you sure you should be at work?'

'I'm perfectly fine. Believe me, it's better than sitting at home, worrying. And I'll be going off on mat leave sooner than planned, so make use of me while you've got me.' God, she hoped she'd be on mat leave. What if she had to leave the hospital without her baby? What would she do then?

'Okay. I guess you're the boss.' Kelly picked up a chart and handed it to her. 'There's a suspected MI in cubicle three.'

Olivia raised her eyebrow as she looked at the notes. Suspected MI, her foot. The patient clearly had little more than indigestion.

She handed the chart back. 'Ask one of the juniors to give him a thorough going over. I need something a bit more challenging.'

Just then the swing doors burst open and the paramedics rushed in, pushing a gurney. A paramedic was on top of the patient, carrying out cardiac massage. Immediately Olivia was alongside, her concentration totally focussed.

'What do we have?' she asked.

That night, Olivia couldn't sleep. With David gone, she felt out of kilter. His restless energy had filled the house, and while it seemed calmer now, it also perversely felt empty and soulless.

It was just that she missed him as a sounding board, she told herself. That was all. In a few short weeks she would be bringing her baby home and there would be no time to feel lonely then. A glow spread through her as she imagined her baby in his crib, the two of them cocooned in the safety of their house.

If she brought him home. With all this silence around her it was impossible not to think about what could happen. Perhaps it was better to prepare herself.

No, she simply could not entertain the thought of a future without her child. So what could she do? A date for the hearing hadn't been set yet. Could she really go through more nights of worry and torment?

She slipped out of bed and into the library. Opening the drawer of the burred oak writing desk, she found what she was looking for. Paper and an envelope. She picked up a pen and started to write.

Dear Dr Carter

I know that I am not supposed to write to you, but I can't not. I feel if only I can make you understand how much this child means to me, you may think again about challenging me for custody in court.

My late husband was diagnosed with a brain tumour around four years ago. We had always wanted children, but I guess, like most couples, we thought we had time. Before he started treatment he donated sperm. Then it looked as if everything was going to be okay when he went into remission, so we went ahead with IVF. Five embryos fertilised, and I had one round of IVF. Sadly the first attempt wasn't successful.

Tears were falling on to the paper smudging her writing. But if she stopped and started again, she didn't know if she would have the courage to finish the letter.

He would have been a great dad.

She got up and stared out of the window towards the Golden Gate Bridge. Richard had worked late every night until he had become ill. Perhaps if he hadn't become ill, he would have carried on working, and perhaps he would have been a distant father. But when he'd realised that he couldn't count on a future, he'd changed. He'd sworn he would scale back his hours so they could spend time as a family. The thought of being a family had been what had kept him strong—kept them both strong—through those dark days.

When the IVF hadn't worked they'd both grieved. And before they could go for the second attempt, Richard's tumour had come back with a vengeance. There had been no room to think about anything else, but Richard had begged her to try with the remaining embryos when he was gone. 'I want to know that you won't be on your own,' he'd said. 'And it helps to know that part of me will still live on in our child.'

But it wasn't his child she was carrying. Nevertheless, she knew Richard would understand how she felt about the baby growing inside her. Had he lived, he would have fought to keep the baby, too.

She went back to her desk and started writing again.

This baby is growing inside me. I can feel him move and I have seen his heartbeat. When I thought I was going to lose him, when he was diagnosed with Hydrops, it was as if someone had turned my world dark again. But the transfusion worked. I will have to have a section in a few weeks' time and until I hold my baby in my arms I won't know if he'll be okay.

But even if he isn't, I will love and treasure him. I will make it my life to make sure that he knows love every day of his life. I will protect and guard him with every part of my being.

I know you want him, too. And I can understand that. If it makes your decision easier, I would be prepared to let you have access. All I truly care about is that my child is loved and knows love.

Tears were flowing down her face. She didn't know what else she could say.

Please, she finished, *I beg you, please don't take my baby.*

David knocked on the door. There was no reply, which was strange as almost every light in the house was on. He hadn't intended to come here when he'd left his new apartment, but somehow his feet had seemed to have a mind of their own. Hadn't he told himself that he'd done everything that could possibly be expected of him? Olivia and her baby were not his problem. No way. Just trouble with a big T. And he didn't do trouble.

But he couldn't stay away. Olivia warmed his world, adding texture and light where there had only been grey before he'd met her. The decorating and furnishing of the nursery had been his attempt to offer practical help, but she was making him believe that he was someone who could feel something. He needed to remember that he couldn't. Not for ever.

He peered in the sitting-room window. No sign of her. Bouncer started barking and wagging his tail.

'Quiet, boy,' he whispered. Bouncer's tail was wagging so hard it was in danger of... Too late. The sculpture on the table crashed to the floor. Immediately Olivia appeared from one of the rooms.

David sucked in a breath. Her pale face was streaked with tears. What had happened? Had she had bad news from the court? Was that why he'd found himself here? He seemed to have developed radar as far as Olivia was concerned—it was as if he knew when she needed him.

The realisation struck him like a tree felled by lightning. He loved this woman. He loved her, despite the fact she was pregnant with someone else's child, despite the fact she was an emotional mess, despite everything. He hadn't wanted it to happen. Damn and double damn. If he was going to fall in love, why couldn't it have been with someone uncomplicated with no emotional baggage? Why hadn't he run in the opposite direction while he could?

Come to think of it, he could still run. She didn't know he was here. He'd be invisible in the darkness. He could find another job in neurosurgery—preferably on the other side of the world. In time he'd forget about her, perhaps meet and fall in love with someone else. Someone. But when she put on the outside light and saw him there, her face lit up and he knew he wasn't going anywhere.

'Don't you have anything better to do?' Olivia asked as she opened the door. 'Or do you stalk all your friends?'

For the first time he could remember David found that his usual ready quip had deserted him.

'I was in the neighbourhood,' he said as she stepped

aside to let him in, 'and thought I'd just see how you were doing.'

'Isn't your new apartment ten miles north of here?' Olivia responded with a quirk of her eyebrow.

Uh-oh. 'I fancied a walk down by the beach,' he said, thinking rapidly. 'Thought you might like to join me.'

'At ten in the evening?'

She was wearing the T-shirt and shorts she usually wore to bed. The T-shirt had ridden up, exposing the mound of her belly. And had her breasts always been as full? He was sure they hadn't. It wasn't the kind of detail he usually missed.

God, now he was feeling all hot and bothered. Was it normal to lust after a pregnant woman? Especially when she was carrying another man's child? None of any of this made any sense. All he knew for certain was that he loved her.

'Means that there's no one about. But if you're ready for bed, I could take Bouncer.'

She smiled. 'I was in bed, but I couldn't sleep. Maybe a walk is just what I need. Wait there while I put some clothes on.' She seemed to suddenly realise that she was wearing next to nothing as she blushed.

She was back in a couple of minutes. He'd never known a woman who could get dressed as quickly as she did. It was another major plus in a long list, as far as he was concerned.

They stepped out into the balmy air, with Bouncer leaping around them in excited circles.

'I suspect he's been moping since you moved out,' Olivia said.

And what about you? David wanted to ask. Have you missed me at all? But he wouldn't ask. She had other stuff to think about.

'How are you?' he asked instead.

'Good. You know, I have the strangest feeling that everything is going to work out.'

'Oh? Did you get something from the lawyers?'

'No. I just have a feeling. Anyway, I've decided that worrying about it can't be good for the baby. Worry never made a problem disappear, so what is the point?'

David wasn't so sure, but it was good to see that she was being strong and brave.

They walked down to the edge of the shore and stood looking out to the lights of the bridge. Unexpectedly, a hand slipped into his, and he squeezed.

'One day I'll bring my son down here,' Olivia said.

'I'm sure you will.'

They stood in silence listening to the gentle lapping of the waves on the shore. 'How's it been?' David asked.

'The media attention? Almost unbearable. Every time I leave the house there's a bunch of reporters waiting to stick a microphone in my face. So I try to avoid going out. I would go to Dad's, but the baby's due another transfusion.'

'Could your dad not come and stay? You have told him what's happening, haven't you?'

'Of course. I could never keep much from him. He was horrified, of course, and offered to come and stay. But to be honest, having Dad to stay would only make everything more complicated. Besides, he has his wedding to plan.'

She sounded so tired David wanted to wrap her in his arms and whisk her away from all of it. Come to think of it, it was a brilliant idea. And he knew just the place.

He took her by the elbow and steered her back up the path. 'You're not working this weekend?' he asked.

'No.'

'Then pack a bag for a couple of nights. We're heading to the mountains.'

CHAPTER THIRTEEN

IT WAS very late by the time they pulled up outside the cabin. David unloaded the car while Olivia took a look around.

As cabins went, this one was luxurious. It had two bedrooms, a bathroom and a sitting room with an enormous fireplace. Outside they could have been in the middle of nowhere: the stars sprinkled the clear night sky, and the full moon gave enough light for them to see without torches. The air up here in the mountains was cooler and crisper than in San Francisco and Olivia drew in deep lungfuls.

'Great, no reporters, no cameras, not even a television,' Olivia said. For the first time since her scan she felt lighter. It might just be for a couple of days, but it was going to be a couple of days when she would put everything that had happened and still might happen to the back of her mind.

David grinned back at her. 'I doubt even the most intrepid of them will find us up here,' he said. He glanced around. 'It's not exactly five stars, is it?'

'I think it's perfect,' Olivia said honestly.

David looked at her and a strange expression crossed his face. 'You really are something else, Dr Simpson. Most women would run a mile.'

'Not me.'

Their eyes locked, and Olivia's heart started galloping.

'Dinner?' she suggested, turning away. 'What have we got?' She unpacked the groceries David had bought on the way and smiled when she noticed the packet of herbal tea. Apart from a bottle of wine and a few beers, he'd bought bread and eggs, cheese, pasta, chicken fillets and a quiche. He'd done well.

She looked at him in surprise. 'I'm impressed,' she said.

'I tried to pick stuff I knew you liked.'

For the first time in weeks Olivia was ravenous.

'Quiche and salad?'

'At this time?'

'I'm starving.'

He laughed. 'Come to think of it, so am I.' He reached behind him and brought out another bag. 'Home-made burgers for me. Doubt I'll ever be able to do the whole quiche thing. I'll do the burgers on the grill outside.'

Once Olivia had prepared the salad she took a beer from the fridge and went outside to join David. He'd made a separate fire and found a couple of chairs.

Olivia handed him the beer, shivering in the cool mountain air.

'Go back inside,' David suggested. 'I can light the fire there.'

'I'd rather be outside. I've spent enough days recently cooped up inside my house.'

When they'd eaten they sat in companionable silence around the fire.

'Tell me more about your family,' Olivia said.

She couldn't read David's expression in the flickering light from the fire.

'You know about Judith.'

'I know that you're not close and that she's an actress. Wasn't she Lydia in the *Miracles of Harrington Road*?' It was a series she used to watch when she'd come to America as a child.

'For the record,' David said harshly, 'Judith is nothing like the character she played in the TV show. My sister has been married three times—or is it four? And has children she rarely sees by each of her husbands. My sister,' David continued, his mouth twisted with distaste, 'will do and say anything to get publicity. She's even touted the fact that I'm a neurosurgeon. She thinks it gives her more kudos with her fans. She's splashed details about our family—personal details that are none of anyone's business—all over the press, and she could even have been responsible for leading the press to your door. Avoiding the media is one of the reasons I stayed with my friend Simon and his wife. If I checked into a hotel I knew they would track me down. They love nothing better than to try and dish up some gossip about anyone connected with Judith. Why anyone should chose to live their life in the public eye escapes me.'

'I'm sorry. Given my recent experience of the press, I know how you feel.' Finally he was sharing some of his life with her, but she wanted to know more. 'What about your brother?'

'Ryan works the club circuit. He's a guitarist in a band.'

'And your other sister?'

'Lisa?' David's voice was low. 'She lives at home.'

'What does she do?'

David stood up and jabbed the fire with a stick. Flames leapt upwards, illuminating his face. Olivia sucked in a breath. She'd never seen David look so closed off before.

'Lisa doesn't—can't—do anything.'

The name sounded familiar but she couldn't remember where she'd heard it before. 'What do you mean?'

When the silence stretched between them, she wondered if David was going to answer her. 'You don't have to tell me if you don't want to,' Olivia said.

'Lisa is a couple of years younger than me. My father is wealthy—extremely wealthy. I only tell you this so you can understand. I guess we all had so much as children, one of us was bound to come unstuck, and that was Lisa. When she was fifteen she fell in with the wrong crowd and started doing drugs. I'm not sure it crossed my parents' minds that there was something up with her. Although I had my own stuff going on—not drugs, I hasten to add, my escape was always sports—I could see that sometimes Lisa was different. All edgy and hyperactive one minute and dopey and subdued the next. Dad was wrapped up in his businesses, and Mother—well, she had her charity work.' There was an edge to David's voice, a bitterness she'd never heard before. 'I tried to ask Lisa, but she always brushed me off. Judith was too focussed on getting her own career off the ground, and Bruce, my younger brother, was only twelve at the time so naturally I couldn't involve him.

'So I tried to help her. But not too hard. By this time I had won a scholarship to college. Believe it or not, at one time I was considering a future in football and the training was tough and all-consuming. At least, that's my excuse.'

'What happened to Lisa, David?' Olivia asked softly.

'Naturally my father had given her a car as soon as she was sixteen. And not just any car. He gave her a

Porsche. We were all given complete freedom to choose our own cars. I suspect giving us whatever we wanted financially made Dad feel better about not spending time at home. Why else would you allow a sixteen-year-old who loves to party that kind of car?'

Although Olivia had already guessed what was coming, she still held her breath.

'Lisa was returning home from a night out. We found out later that she was high on a cocktail of drugs. She went off the road—thankfully no other cars were involved—and crashed into a tree. Luckily a passing motorist saw the accident and called 911. She was asystolic when the paramedics arrived but they got her heart going. She was taken to hospital where they worked on her.'

David looked off into the distance. A coyote howled, but apart from its mournful cry the only other sound was the snap and spit of the fire.

'They saved her life, but Lisa was in a deep coma for weeks. My mother was distraught. She blamed herself, and she was right. But instead of the accident bringing us closer, my parents withdrew even more from us. I guess Dad felt guilty too, but if I thought he would start spending time with his family I was mistaken.'

David's voice was rough. He laughed shortly. 'The press had a field day, as you can imagine. Every sordid detail about the accident—and anything else they could turn up—was published in the press. I swear Judith used it to advance her career. After a while Lisa came out of the coma and I thought I would get my sister back. But the brain injury was too severe. My sister will never walk or talk again. At least not without the help of her specially adapted computer.'

Olivia reached out and took David's hand.

'Where is she now?'

'At home. With round-the-clock carers. It was one thing my parents could do, although I suspect that if my father could have left her in some sort of long-term institution he would have. My father wanted the perfect family, so I imagine seeing Lisa every day was a reminder that he didn't want. Soon after she came home, he left. I don't see him, and I won't touch a cent of his money.'

'I'm so sorry, David.'

David let her hand go and stood, thrusting his hands deep into his pocket. 'Families, huh. I don't get why people are so keen to marry. My sister has had several husbands, and my brother's had two wives. Little sis is the only one anyone could describe as being close to normal. The only one in my family I care anything for.'

His story explained a lot that Olivia had been wondering about. No wonder he played the field.

'Is that why you went into neurosurgery?' she asked.

'Oh, the bit about the Meccano is true too. But, yes. Up until my sister's accident I was going to try to become an athlete. If I couldn't make it I was going to join Dad in the family business. But then I decided what the hell—I owed him nothing. In that respect Lisa's accident and my father's behaviour afterwards helped me discover what I really wanted from life. I was clear from that point on I was going to be a doctor.' His face softened into a smile. 'And that was the best decision I've ever made.'

As she studied him, Olivia knew without a shadow of a doubt that she had fallen deeply and irrevocably in love with the man sitting opposite her, and the realisation filled her with dismay. She needed to get away from him before he saw it in her eyes.

She stumbled to her feet. 'I think I'll go to bed now.'

After Olivia had gone to bed, David sat by the fire

with a drink in his hand. He felt odd. He'd never spoken to anyone about Lisa before, or about his dysfunctional family. In fact, it had taken him years to realise just how dysfunctional they were. Until then he'd thought all families were like that. No wonder he preferred to keep his life unencumbered.

How, then, had he managed to fall so hard for Olivia? Her life couldn't be more complicated. He knew that, so he should have stayed away.

He should still keep away from her. There was an attending post that had unexpectedly become available in New York. He would apply for it, and as soon as Olivia's baby was born he could go back to the life he liked. Work, dating beautiful, simple women, going to football games with his friends.

Why, then, did it all seem kind of empty?

Olivia stretched languorously. Daylight was streaming through the window and the sound of someone chopping wood with a steady rhythm came from outside.

The baby moved, and she placed her hands on her tummy. 'Hey, you hang on in there,' she whispered. 'You're doing fine. Just fine.'

She slipped out of bed and pulled a cashmere cardigan on over her pyjamas. In the kitchen she boiled the kettle and spooned some instant coffee into a mug for David and dipped a rosehip teabag for herself.

Then she stuck her feet into her boots and carried the mugs outside.

David was too busy chopping wood to notice her. Dressed in a pair of jeans and a sleeveless T-shirt, he swung the axe with effortless ease. She leaned against the doorjamb, enjoying the chance to watch him unobserved. She was glad he'd shared his story with her last night. Now she knew what drove him, he appealed to her even more. No wonder he didn't want to get married or have children.

David put down the axe with a satisfied grunt and looked up to see her standing there.

She held out the mug of coffee. 'I thought you might need this.'

His eyes glittered. 'Did I ever tell you that you are practically perfect, Dr Simpson?'

Perfect, yes, Olivia thought grumpily, because he didn't see her as a woman. More like a best mate, albeit one with a mountain of problems.

What would have happened had she met David before she'd gone ahead with the implantation? But she couldn't think that way. She wanted this baby, and even with all the trauma of knowing she might lose him, she couldn't regret it. She pushed the thought away. She'd promised that for these two days she wasn't going to think about the possibility. No—she was going to pretend that her baby was safe and healthy and there was no chance of him being taken from her.

As for David… She smiled to herself. She was going to make the most of being here with him. For two days, just two days, she was going to pretend everything in her world was hunky-dory.

'What would you like to do today?' David asked.

'I'm easy,' she said, and felt the colour rise to her cheeks as soon as she'd said the words. 'I mean, I'm happy to do anything as long as it's not too energetic.

David grinned and her heart turned over. 'Never thought you were easy,' he said. 'What about a swim? There's a lake a short hike away.'

'It's a bit chilly for a swim.' Olivia replied. 'Even if I'd brought my bathing suit,' she said, 'but you go ahead.'

'Come to think of it, I didn't bring mine either, but I'm not going to let that stop me.'

'How far away is this lake? Even if I'm not swimming, I could come with you.'

'A couple of miles up the road. Not far. Are you up to the walk?'

She felt okay. The next transfusion wasn't due for a week and no doubt she'd feel ropier as the time for it drew closer, but right now she had never felt healthier.

'Definitely,' Olivia said. 'Just let me pack a picnic and my book.'

By the time they were organised, the sun was high in the sky and it was pleasantly warm. They walked side by side, David shortening his stride to match hers and pausing every now and again to push an intruding branch out of her path.

Without warning they burst into a clearing and there before them was the lake. On the other side a small waterfall gushed into the deep blue water. Apart from the gurgling of the water and the calls of the birds there was silence. All the tension that had been building up inside Olivia melted away.

'What do you think?'

'I think it's wonderful. How did you know it was here?'

'I looked at the map. You know those things you can buy that have squiggles and lines and tell you where things are?'

'Ha! How droll.'

Olivia set out a blanket on the ground and David set the backpack with their picnic down. Then he pulled his dark grey T-shirt over his head. Olivia averted her eyes, but not before she had caught a glimpse of his tanned chest and hard-muscled stomach.

She pretended to busy herself removing items from the bag. She heard the zipper of his jeans come down, and a short while later a splash.

Finally allowing herself to look, she saw David swimming across to the waterfall with fast, powerful strokes. She watched him for a while, before getting her book out and lying back to read.

David swam a few lengths of the lake before easing himself out of the water. He walked naked across to the towel he'd left by the side of the lake and towelled himself dry. When he picked up his jeans to pull them on, he noticed that Olivia had fallen asleep still with her book in her hand. He glanced at the cover. *You and Your Baby.* Grimacing, he tossed the book aside and stretched out on his side beside her. In sleep she looked vulnerable. Her mouth was turned up slightly at the corners as if she was dreaming of something pleasant. Her chest was rising and falling and her T-shirt had ridden up slightly, exposing the taut, rounded mound of her pregnancy.

Her legs, protruding from her tiny shorts, were crossed at the ankles. Did she have any idea how great her legs were? Did she have any idea how beautiful she was? She was unlike any woman he'd dated. They were always very sure of their beauty but, despite that, seemed to want constant reassurances. Olivia, on the other hand, was very comfortable with herself, and with the way she looked. In that she was a complete novelty. No wonder he loved her.

Her eyelids flickered and he found himself staring into her dark green eyes.

She stretched lazily. 'Hello, have I been asleep for long?'

He took a blade of grass and stuck it in his mouth, chewing hard to stop the words that rose to his lips.

She sat up and pushed back her blonde hair. 'Are you ready for something to eat?'

If only she knew. Food was the last thing on his mind.

Olivia passed the bread for David to cut. It was odd how right it felt, the pair of them being here. But why was he here? He'd made it very clear that he wasn't interested in getting caught up in other people's lives.

'David?' she asked as she passed him a slice of cheese. 'Hmm?'

'I want to ask you something.'

He looked over at her with a guarded expression.

'Sure. Fire away.'

'Why are you doing all this? I mean, you must have better things to do with your time. Women to see, games to go to…your sister…'

'You were in trouble,' he said.

'But it's not as if you owe me anything. I'm a comparative stranger after all.'

He finished putting the cheese on the bread and passed it back to her.

'People don't always have to do something for a reason, do they? I assume you'd do the same if someone needed your help.'

She couldn't help but feel disappointed. But what had she expected him to say?

'Besides, I like women.'

Olivia raised an eyebrow. 'Do you?'

He looked taken aback. 'Of course. I enjoy their company. I enjoy taking them out and…you know.' He grinned wickedly.

'That's not quite the same thing. Do you have women friends?'

David looked genuinely shocked. 'I do.'

'Who?'

'Well, there's a colleague from New York. We used to meet sometimes. And there's...' He tailed off.

'See! How many of the women you've dated would you actually be friends with?'

'Well, not Melissa for a start. Look, I know what you thought that evening at your place, but I really didn't invite her over. She's just wouldn't take no for an answer.'

Silence fell between them.

'And the woman you go to see every second weekend in New York?' Suddenly realisation struck. 'It's Lisa, isn't it? That's who you've been seeing.'

'Of course. Who else?' His eyes held hers. 'You really thought I'd been dating people here while I had someone else in New York? Shame on you!'

Olivia flushed. Inside she felt a thrill of delight.

'Enough about me,' David said lazily. 'Let's talk about you instead.'

'No. Let's not. Just for these next couple of days I want to pretend...' She wanted to pretend that there was nothing wrong with her world. She wanted to pretend that she was a woman looking forward to the birth of her baby. She wanted to pretend that she was with the man she loved and who loved her in return...but of course she couldn't tell him the last part. 'To pretend that everything is okay in my world,' she finished lamely.

'We can do that,' he said softly. He traced the curve of her cheek with his fingertip and a shiver ran all the way down her spine to her pelvis. He tipped her face towards him and she held her breath. His lips touched hers. It was no more than the lightest of touches, but her bones seemed to melt. She swayed towards him but he pulled away and looked up at the sky. 'I think there's rain on the way,' he said roughly. 'We'd better get back.'

Back in the cabin, Olivia took her book and settled

on the couch to read while David prowled around like an animal in a cage.

Finally, just when she was going to tell him that she couldn't read with him pacing up and down (not that she was really reading, the book just gave her something to hide behind), he pulled on a pair of boots.

'I think I'll go for a walk. There's a ridge a couple of miles away. I'd like to see what's on the other side.'

'But it's raining,' she protested.

'A little bit of rain isn't going to bother me.'

Olivia's heart sank. He was bored. He was only here because of her and it couldn't be clearer that he wished himself anywhere else.

He finished tying his laces. 'Will you be okay for a while? I'll only be an hour or two.'

'Sure. I have my book.'

'I'll take my phone. If you need me, call.'

'I won't need you,' she replied.

Almost before she had finished speaking he was out of the door.

When he'd left, Olivia gave up pretending to read and crossed over to the window. Already David was almost out of sight.

She peeled some vegetables and chopped up some chicken to make a casserole and popped it in the oven. Then she wandered around the cabin for a bit. She thought about taking a bath, but she'd already showered. A rumble of thunder in the distance worried her. When she looked out of the window the rain was falling in earnest. David would get soaked but, then, as he'd said, getting wet was hardly likely to affect someone in his peak condition. The image of him pulling off his T-shirt flashed into her mind. As if she didn't have enough to worry about! How had she managed to let herself fall in love with a man who couldn't have made it clearer that he wasn't into long-term relationships or children? Never mind another man's child. And as she would never bring a man into her child's life who wasn't one hundred per cent committed to them both, any possible future for her and David was a non-starter.

But she couldn't help the way she felt. It wasn't as if her brain and her heart were talking to each other. Quite the opposite. They appeared to be completely separate.

Anyway, why had she fallen for David? *Girl, you sure have found yourself trouble.*

She returned to her book, trying not to think. And trying to ignore the fact that the thunder was getting closer and the rain harder. Where was he? How long did it take to climb a ridge and back? She got out the map and traced the route with her finger. In her pre-pregnancy days she would have done it in a couple of hours, tops. Yet David had been gone longer than that. Had something happened to him? Had he fallen and was now lying somewhere? There were bears in this part of the country. Was it possible he'd come across one?

She tried his phone but it went to voice mail. Looking at the signal strength on hers, she saw it was down to one bar. Damn.

She decided to give him another thirty minutes. If he wasn't back by then, she would decide what to do.

In the meantime, she went out onto the porch and scanned the horizon. She couldn't see for the trees so she walked a little distance from the cabin. Within a few moments she was soaked.

She hesitated. Another ten minutes and she would need to do something. Either try to follow the path he'd taken to the ridge or go for help. She'd have to take the car as they were a good forty miles from civilisation.

The rain was falling harder now, plastering her dress to her body and her hair to her scalp.

She shouldn't stay out here much longer. But she couldn't bring herself to go back into the cabin.

Just as she was about to give up, she saw a figure appear from the woods and David emerged. He was sauntering along. There was clearly nothing wrong with him. He'd let her worry and fret for nothing.

It was as if the weeks of worry and confusion were like a volcano inside her ready to explode.

'Where the hell have you been?' she demanded as he loped towards her. Part of her took in the way his wet T-shirt clung to him, emphasising the muscles of his arms and chest.

David frowned. 'For a hike. As I said.' He stepped closer and concern darkened his eyes. 'What are you doing out here? You're soaked.'

'I was looking for you. I thought...' Her words tailed away as David grabbed her by the arm.

'Explanations can wait. Let's get you inside and out of those clothes.'

Olivia tried to dig her heels in but he was too strong. Before she knew it she had been whisked inside and David was rubbing her hair with a towel.

'I was worried!' It was difficult to maintain the moral high ground when he was drying her off like a child and parts of the towel were falling over her eyes, making it difficult to see.

He stopped drying for a moment and peered down at her. 'You were really worried, weren't you?' His mouth twitched. 'What did you think had happened to me? That I had been eaten by a bear?'

She wasn't going to tell him that that was only one of the things she'd been thinking. Now he was here, her fevered imaginings seemed so crazy. Could he really blame her? Who would have imagined, for example, that she would discover that the baby she was carrying wasn't her genetic child?

David walked into the bathroom and started running the bath.

Olivia stalked after him—or at least waddled after him, as the size of her abdomen meant it was the only way she could move.

'So that's it?' she demanded. 'You were away for ages, far longer than I expected you to be, and now you're just going to take a bath and pretend that nothing happened?' She just couldn't stop the words pouring from her mouth. She wasn't his minder. She was nothing more than an inconvenience to him.

Fury erupted again. 'Take me home,' she demanded. 'Right now.'

He looked at her and his eyes crinkled at the corners. 'I didn't know you had a temper,' he said calmly. 'But we're not going anywhere. These roads will be impassable in an hour, and at least until morning. And by the way, this bath is not for me. It's for you. Now lift your arms above your head so I can get you out of these wet clothes.'

'I do not want a bath.' Her teeth were chattering— whether it was from the cold or anger she didn't know. 'And I'm perfectly able to undress myself. My God, David, do you think I'm unable to do anything?'

But he wasn't listening. Instead, he lifted one hand above her head and raised her T-shirt. Now she couldn't see him again as it was obscuring her view. She tried to pull it back down but he was far stronger than her. Before she knew it her T-shirt was lying on the floor and he was tugging at the zip on her shorts.

'One more move and I'll sock you,' she warned. 'Trust me. I'll sock you.'

To her fury he laughed. 'Then you take them off, because if you don't, trust me, I will.'

She felt totally ridiculous standing there in nothing but her bra and her shorts, but the glint in his eye told her that he would do exactly as he said.

Then, before she knew it, she was laughing. Then suddenly she was crying and he was holding her, stroking her wet hair. His T-shirt was damp against her cheek, but through the wetness she could feel his heat.

He just held her.

Eventually she pulled away. 'Sorry,' she sniffed.

Very gently, he eased off her shorts and her underwear and helped her into the bath. She felt no embarrassment, only deep weariness.

He washed her back and then her hair. Once he'd finished he held out his hand and helped her out. Wrapping her up, he carried her to the sitting room and sat her in one of the chairs. With a fresh towel he dried each foot. After that he towel-dried her hair before doing each arm and moving to her legs. Olivia closed her eyes as she felt the material on her calves then on her thighs. He paused and looked at her.

'Do you want me to continue?' His voice was husky.

She nodded. She was burning with her need for him to keep touching her. If he stopped now, she would explode. Her body was tingling from the roots of her hair to the nails on her toes. Every bit of her skin felt as if it had an electric current running over it.

When she felt his hands move further up, she parted her legs slightly to allow him access. There was no longer any pretence that he was drying her.

His hands on the tops of her thighs were cool and she gasped as he touched her. A shock wave ran through her body. She knew she should stop. What she was doing—what she was allowing him to do—was crazy. But her need was too strong. She couldn't have stopped him if her life depended on it.

When he touched her she was wet and aching. She arched her hips, allowing him better access. She could feel his fingers on her, inside her, and suddenly, without warning, she came in an explosion that made her feel as if she had spiralled off to another planet.

When she finally opened her eyes it was to find him looking at her. The look in her eyes told her he wanted her as much as she wanted him, as much as she still wanted him. This time it was her hands that were tugging at the button of his jeans. Her hands that were on his zipper, pulling his jeans over his thighs. When he was naked, he leaned forward and stared deeply into her eyes. 'We don't have to,' he said.

'I want to. Please don't argue with me this time.' She smiled slightly to let him know that she meant it. With her still sitting on the chair and him kneeling in front of her, he slipped his hands under her bottom and dropped his mouth to kiss her breasts and the mound of her stomach. She wrapped her hands in his hair, pulling him closer. Within minutes she was ready for him again and she dropped her hands to his hips, signalling her need to feel him inside her.

When he finally entered her, his skin smooth as silk, she gasped. It felt so right, so goddamn right. As they moved in unison wave upon wave of pleasure coursed through her body and she closed her eyes, glad to be taken back to oblivion.

* * *

Later, when they were lying in bed—how they had got there Olivia wasn't at all sure—she snuggled into him. Her head was lying on his chest, his fingers still wrapped in her hair. Right now, safe in the cocoon of the cabin, she felt happy and content.

'Are you awake? David murmured.

'No,' she replied with a smile. 'Idiot.'

The smell of burning drifted into the room and within seconds they were both out of bed.

'Damn! The casserole,' Olivia said. She'd totally forgotten that she'd put it in the oven. David raced to the kitchen while Olivia slipped into one of his dry T-shirts, and followed at a necessarily slower pace behind.

David was flicking his fingers and the casserole was sitting on the kitchen counter, smelling decidedly burnt.

'I hope you weren't hungry,' she said.

'I'm starving, woman. Sex always does that to me.'

Olivia lowered her eyes as images of what they'd been doing flashed back into her head. It seemed that the same thoughts had been going through David's head as he took her by the hand. 'But not so hungry that I can't wait until later.'

Much later, as they lay in each other's arms, Olivia's mind turned back to her baby.

'I wish I could freeze time,' she said, 'and forget that in a couple of weeks I might have to give up my baby.'

'I don't think it will come to that.'

'Why not? The last time I met with my lawyer she asked me all sorts of questions. Was I dating? What did I intend to do about work when the baby was born? Did I get on with my mother as a child? It was as if I was on trial!'

'What did you tell her?'

'The truth. I wasn't dating. I hoped to go back to work when my baby was old enough. I had a very good relationship with my mother before she died. My childhood was happy. She asked about you. Were we a couple? Did we have plans?'

'She asked about me?'

'Yes. She seemed to think that if we were seeing each other in a—you know—serious way, that might help my case.'

She felt rather than heard his sharp intake of breath.

'And what did you say to that?'

'I told him we were friends and colleagues, nothing more. That's the truth, isn't it?'

She shifted until she could see his face. But there was nothing she could read in his guarded expression except possibly relief.

'I don't pretend to think that what happened here means anything, David,' she said, forcing her voice to sound light. 'It was...' She struggled to find the right word. 'It was amazing and...' God, where was her power of speech when she needed it? 'It was amazing and it helped me forget for a while, but it's not real. I know that.'

'I'm glad you feel that way too,' he said finally. 'I like you—a lot. But you know I'm not looking for a permanent relationship.'

Especially not with a woman whose life is as complicated as mine, Olivia finished the sentence in her head. She wished he felt differently. She wished he would think of giving them a chance. It wasn't as if she were in a hurry to marry again, but maybe one day. Unfortunately David couldn't have made it clearer that that one day was never going to come for him.

She couldn't be angry. He had never pretended to

feel more than he did, she had been more than a willing participant in their lovemaking. Neither could she regret it. All she regretted was that soon he would be out of her life. Because she knew deep in her soul that one day soon he would be.

Later, they picnicked in front of the fire on more bread and cheese. They talked about work and places they had been, both carefully avoiding the subject of what had just happened. When they'd finished eating they went back to bed and fell asleep in each other's arms.

David looked at the sleeping woman beside him. What had he done? Why the hell couldn't he keep it in his pants?

Of all the women to have seduced, why couldn't he have kept his hands off this one?

She needed him in her life like a hole in the head.

What the hell was he going to do now?

Very gently he extracted himself from her arms and slipped out of bed. He pulled on his jeans and stepped outside.

The full moon cast a silvery light on the ground and lit up the area as if it were a thousand-watt bulb.

David thought he saw something move in the trees. He stepped closer, trying to see what it was. A bear perhaps? Had they inadvertently left something around that had attracted its attention?

But as he stared into the trees something flashed and his blood ran cold. That was no bear. That was a man—or woman—with a camera. Whoever it was must have realised that they'd been spotted as they turned and began to run back along the track leading to the cabin.

He ran across the open ground after the figure. Whoever it was couldn't have been used to doing much exercise as when David caught up with him his car was still a few metres away and he was bending over, clutching his knees and wheezing.

'Who the hell are you?' David said, reaching for the camera and taking it from the man's unprotesting hands.

'I'm Linus Filbert.' He made a feeble effort to grab his camera back.

'Are you a reporter?' David was furious. He'd been papped before and knew the lengths journalists would go to get a story, but for someone to follow them up here in an attempt to get more out of Olivia's pain was unforgivable.

'Give me the film,' David said.

'No can do, I'm sorry. Didn't manage to get a photo of her yet anyway. You spotted me before I could get one.'

David closed his eyes in relief. While he'd been chasing the man the thought that he'd taken a photo of them making love had crossed his mind. He couldn't even begin to imagine how mortified Olivia would be to see that sort of photograph splashed across the paper.

'Anyway, it's you I want to know more about.'

'Me?'

'I saw your picture in the paper and I recognised you straight away. You're part of the Stuart family, aren't you? Now, what is someone like you doing with Dr Olivia Simpson?'

Furious, David grabbed a fistful of Linus's shirt. 'What the hell has that got to do with you?'

Linus looked frightened. 'If I were you I'd keep my hands to myself. You wouldn't want anyone to know that Dr Olivia Simpson, the disputed mother of her unborn child, is having an affair with a man with violent tendencies, would you? I can't see any judge wanting to give custody to someone with a person like that in their life, can you?'

David let him go—what other option did he have? He watched Linus drive away, waiting until the sound of his car faded into the distance.

In all of this he'd been resisting getting involved with Olivia because he didn't want complications in his life. Yet here he was, *bringing* trouble. The press had probably picked up on her story because of who he was—or rather who his sister was—and now the opposing lawyers believed their case was stronger because of him. He'd been a fool. An unthinking fool. All he'd done had been to make everything worse for the woman he loved.

CHAPTER FOURTEEN

WHEN Olivia woke again the sun was streaming through the window and the space beside her empty. She glanced at her watch. Nine o'clock! She couldn't remember the last time she had slept so late. She padded through to the kitchen and found it empty too. Perhaps David had headed out for another hike before breakfast? She couldn't blame him. The sun was beating down and all signs of the previous night's rain had evaporated.

She fixed herself a mug of tea and wandered outside. The boot of the car was open and David was placing his bag inside.

'Morning,' she said, puzzled. They weren't due to leave until later in the afternoon. 'A bit early to be packing.'

'Something's come up with one of my patients. He'd decided to be undecided about the operation he's to have. I need to get back to the city so I can speak to him.'

'Sure,' Olivia said. Patients sometimes had second thoughts about operations and wanted to go over the reasons and risks with the surgeon one final time, but there was something in the way David wasn't quite meeting her eyes that chilled her.

'I'll go and get my stuff together.'

David smiled briefly and turned his attention back to the car.

As she showered, Olivia felt sick. Although she had no reason to think that the story about the patient wasn't true, that didn't explain David's coolness towards her. His manner couldn't be more different from last night.

Had last night, their lovemaking, been all about sympathy and pity? Had he simply not known what to do with a crying, distressed woman except make love to her, and now he was panicking in case she read more into it than he'd intended?

She was embarrassed, but deep down she couldn't help but smile. What did she expect? She was a woman thirty-two weeks pregnant with a baby that was genetically not hers or her late husband's. The father of that baby was trying to take the baby from her, and even if she did win custody, her child could still have medical problems. If there was a description written down somewhere of the kind of woman who would not appeal to David, she was it.

She had gone through a complete meltdown last night. It would be the last. She might love David but she needed to do this on her own. The last thing she wanted was for him to hang about because he felt responsible for her. That was too humiliating.

From here on out, she would do it by herself. She didn't need anyone's help. The fight was hers and hers alone. Tomorrow her baby would have its final transfusion, two weeks later her baby would be born and… This was the part that she couldn't get past. The part where she had no idea. But she was damned if she was going to sit back and leave it to the lawyers any more. This was her child and she would do everything in her power to bring him home.

The car ride back to the city was miserable, with neither of them speaking much.

When they arrived at her house she waited until David retrieved her bag from the boot.

'Thanks for the trip,' she said lightly. 'It was fun. But, you know, David, I don't think we should see each other again—at least outside work.'

Her heart splintered as she saw the look of relief in his eyes. But it gave her the strength to continue. 'I'm really worried that Dr Carter's attorneys might use our—um—friendship to damage my case and I really can't take the risk.'

'Of course not,' David said stiffly. He brushed her cheek with the back of his hand. 'Take care, sweetheart. Let me know how it goes.' Then, without a backward glance, he jumped back into the car and drove away and out of her life.

Olivia let herself in, her throat tight with tears. She wouldn't think about David. She couldn't. Instead she went immediately to the nursery. The cot was in place, a coloured mobile hanging over the rails. Toys were placed on the chair beside the cot and the changing table was laid out with nappies. Would her baby even see this room? Would she ever sit in the chair, nursing her child? She knew that if she lost her baby she could never return to this house.

She could lose her baby.

She went to the study and took a sheet of paper from the drawer. Although Dr Carter hadn't even acknowledged the letter she'd sent him, writing it had made her feel better. If she was going to lose her baby, she had to let her child know that it hadn't been her decision. She didn't know what else to do so she started to write a letter to the son she knew she might never hold.

CHAPTER FIFTEEN

A FEW days later Olivia met with her attorney.

'Dr Carter is still seeking custody,' said Olivia's lawyer, a smart-as-a-whip graduate from Harvard. 'In fact, I'm sorry to tell you he's started playing dirty.'

'In what way?' Olivia's heart thudded against her ribs.

'Although he's pursuing the angle that the baby is his genetically and legally, he's also going for the angle that you're a single mother in a relationship with someone who—if the relationship continues—might become the father, so to speak, of his baby. Their lawyer has found it difficult to attack you—as you say, there are few if any skeletons in your cupboard. But Dr Stuart is a different story. There are more skeletons in his cupboard than in a graveyard.'

'David? What relationship?'

'They apparently have evidence that you spent last weekend with him. I'm sorry, it seems that Dr Carter employed a private detective to dig up any dirt on you that they could. I suspect you've been watched pretty much since Dr Carter found out about the baby.'

Olivia closed her eyes. This was the man who was trying to take her baby away from her? Not a decent man, as she'd thought, but someone who would stoop to any means to get his child, whatever the cost. Her mouth felt as if it was filled with ashes. She'd been followed and spied on.

No wonder David had run a mile. He was being investigated too, although none of this had anything to do with him.

'What skeletons?' Olivia asked.

'Well, perhaps not so much about him—although they will pinpoint his unreliable history as far as relationships are concerned—but about his family. There are bound to be secrets that his sister has.'

'But what has his sister's private life to do with me and my baby? I haven't even met her!'

'There's another sister too. One that the family rarely sees. Apparently she has a brain injury after being in a car accident that apparently was caused by the driver of the car being under the influence of drugs.'

'But all this is rubbish! I mean, part of it is true, but it has nothing to do with me and my baby. Dr Stuart and I are not in a relationship, never were and never will be. He has nothing, I repeat nothing, to do with this, and his family has even less.'

'We could get our own private detective and go after John Carter,' Abigail said quietly. 'He's bound to have secrets too. We know he's moved the egg donor into his home, we know he tracked her down. That behaviour is, if not unethical, then certainly skirting it.'

'No,' Olivia said. 'I won't go down that route. This is unsavoury enough as it is. Whatever happens to my child, my son, whoever he ends up with, I don't want him reading stuff about anyone important in his life that will cause him one minute of anxiety or concern. I don't care what this Dr Carter is up to, but I won't be part of it. My baby, my child, belongs with me. Anybody should be able to see that. And if the worst happens and I lose custody…' she took a deep breath, trying to steady her voice '…I would rather my child goes to his biological father than to foster-parents. I believe—I know—that the best thing for Josh is to be with me. All you and I need to do is make the judge believe it too.'

After she left the lawyer's office, she phoned David and asked him to meet her. He had the right to know what was happening. She shuddered with revulsion. She hated it that she had unwittingly dragged him into this.

He had just come out of surgery and still had patients to see, so they agreed to meet that evening at Olivia's house. As soon as he'd established that there was nothing wrong with her or the baby, he sounded wary. Too bad. This wasn't something they could talk about over the phone.

Despite everything, the sound of his voice on the phone made her knees feel weak.

She was waiting at the window when he came in later without knocking. She hadn't seen him since that morning they'd left the cabin and as soon as she saw him she was transported back to that night. The night when she'd come so close to believing that he loved her. As she loved him.

He was dressed all in black—black jeans, black T-shirt—the darkness of his clothes only serving to highlight the silvery glint in his eyes.

He wasn't smiling. If anything, he looked ill at ease. Olivia had never seen him anything but supremely confident, and it shook her. Did he think she'd invited him here because she wanted to make some claim on him? Didn't he know she would rather live the rest of her life without him than have him resent a single moment with her?

'Please, David, sit down—you're making me nervous.'

'I shouldn't be here,' David said. 'It will only make everything worse for you.'

'That's what I wanted to warn you about. My attorney has just let me know that Dr Carter's legal team are looking into your family. I'm so sorry. I had no idea that you'd be dragged into all of this.'

'You dragging me?' David raised his eyebrows. 'God, Olivia, surely you know it's the other way round? It was me who brought the press to your door in the first place.'

'You don't know that for sure,' Olivia protested.

'No, I don't. But it makes sense. Stupidly I didn't think of the effect it would have on you. I'm used to the press and used to their lies, I should have guessed that they would use you, use us, to dish more dirt on me and my family. It never crossed my mind either that the other side would use what the press knew about me and try to use what they had on me to damage your case.'

He sighed. 'I should have told you that I caught a private detective spying on us when we were up at the cabin. I thought if I stopped having anything to do with you they would turn their attention away from you and back to me. It was a crazy idea.' He grinned tiredly, and Olivia caught her breath. This was the grin she'd fallen for all those weeks ago. And he'd been keeping away from her to try and protect her. At least, that was one of the reasons.

'Do you have any idea how hard it's been for me to stay away from you?' he asked. 'Knowing that you've been here on your own, not knowing what's happening, except through texts…'

'You don't have to stay away,' she said softly.

'I do,' he said. He hesitated. 'I should tell you. I'm

thinking of going back to New York. An attending position has opened up and if they offer me the post, I'm going to take it.'

CHAPTER SIXTEEN

THE second transfusion wasn't quite as fraught as the first. Nevertheless, Olivia was hugely relieved when it went without a hitch. And finally the day she'd been both longing for and dreading was finally here. The day when her baby would be delivered. She refused to think about what might happen afterwards. There had still been no reply to her letter to John Carter, and his lawyer was still pursuing custody on his behalf.

At least there was no danger of her son being taken out of her arms and placed into foster-care. The baby would require another final transfusion as soon as he was born—this one carrying less risk than the in utero transfusions, and then, because of his gestation, her baby would need a minimum of two weeks in the nursery. Whatever happened, she would at least have that time with her child.

She hadn't seen David since the evening he'd come to her house, but he sent her texts most days asking her how she was. She kept her replies short and casual.

When they came to take her to Theatre she gripped the theatre nurse's hand.

Thirty minutes later her baby had been delivered. The doctor showed him to her briefly before handing him over to the paediatricians. She had only enough time to register dark hair.

'We'll let you hold him once we transfuse him,' the midwife said. 'But he looks in better shape then we hoped.'

Every fibre of her being longed to hold her baby and it was almost unbearable when Josh cried out as they stuck a needle in his arm. Poor mite. What a welcome to the world. He should be being held against her, wrapped in the safety of her arms, yet she couldn't even comfort him when he was in pain. Moments later, they whisked him away to the special care nursery.

For the time being she had to let Dr Washington close her wound and trust the paediatricians to do their job. She kept telling herself that all that mattered was that Josh would be well. She had to hold onto that. She closed her eyes, trying to imprint the brief glimpse of Josh on her memory, and breathed a silent prayer. *Please, God, if you're there, look after my baby.*

When she woke her room was dark except for the dim light from the ward. Kelly was sitting by her chair and as soon as she saw that Olivia was awake she jumped to her feet.

'Josh?' Olivia asked. 'How is he?'

'He's doing well. We can go and see him upstairs if you like. I'll fetch a wheelchair for you.'

The relief robbed her of her breath. She could bear almost anything if she knew her child was healthy.

'I can walk,' Olivia protested, but when she tried to get out of bed, the pain from the wound in her abdomen made her grit her teeth.

'I'll go and get a chair, shall I?' Kelly said with a grin.

'But while I'm doing that, there's someone who would like to see you.'

Olivia's heart leaped. Was it David? But when Kelly opened the door it was to reveal Olivia's lawyer. She felt dizzy. Was she coming to tell her that she couldn't see her baby until a decision had been made?

But Abigail was holding an enormous bouquet of flowers and grinning from ear to ear.

'Congratulations! You have a baby son!'

'I do know what sex my child is,' Olivia said dryly. 'But thanks. I'm about to go and see him. They tell me he's going to be fine. You should let Dr Carter know.'

'No,' Abigail said. 'I mean you have a son. Truly. He's all yours. I've just got off the phone to Dr Carter's lawyers and they tell me he's decided to withdraw his claim for custody. We need to get his signature and a few other details need to be ironed out—but basically Josh is yours. For keeps.'

This time Olivia's legs did give way. Luckily Kelly had returned from wherever she'd gone with the wheelchair and had it positioned right behind Olivia.

'You mean it? He's really decided not to fight? Josh is to stay with me?'

'Yes. I spoke to him myself. If he can see the child sometimes, he'd be grateful, but he's decided that it is in Josh's best interests to be with you. I gather you wrote to him.' Abigail frowned slightly. 'I wouldn't ever recommend that course of action—the courts wouldn't have approved of you approaching him—but in this case, whatever you said to Dr Carter seems to have struck home. He says that he didn't receive your letter until yesterday, otherwise he would have let you know before now, but, as it is, he's incredibly relieved that Josh is okay and he wants you to stop worrying that you will lose him. He says in time perhaps you'll meet. Dr Carter also wants to apologise for the intrusion into your life by the PI his attorney hired. He asks me to tell you that he's appalled that the PI went beyond his remit.'

'Can I see my baby?' Olivia couldn't think about meeting Josh's biological father right now. Right now she needed to hold her son.

The special care nursery was dimly lit, with nightlights around each cot. There were several doctors and nurses around some of the cots, working over their tiny occupants.

Olivia was shocked to see a familiar figure bending over one particular cot. It was David.

'What's he doing here?' she whispered to Kelly.

'Not a clue,' Kelly said. 'But that's Josh he's with.'

Kelly pushed Olivia over to her baby. As she looked down on her little son her throat closed. He was so small. So unbelievably, heartbreakingly small. But he was alive. Surrounded by bright blue lights, his eyes covered against the glare, she could only see his limbs and his tiny chest rising and falling as he breathed. But there was no evidence of any oedema that would suggest he was still anaemic.

David turned when he saw her. 'Olivia!'

'What are you doing here, David?' she asked quietly. She reached her hand through the hole in the incubator and placed her finger in her son's minute hand. Immediately his fingers tightened around hers. Her arms ached with the need to hold her baby but she knew it could be days, weeks even before she could hold him in her arms.

'Isn't he beautiful?' she breathed.

And he was. He had a shock of dark hair and his tiny

rosebud mouth was pursed as if he was dreaming. He stretched out, throwing his arms to the side. Olivia tried not to see how small his limbs were.

'He'll grow stronger every day,' David said softly. 'The nurses tell me he's a fighter.' A brief smile crossed his face. 'Like his mother.'

'You didn't say what you were doing here,' Olivia whispered. 'I thought you'd be on your way to New York by now.'

'I couldn't leave,' David said. 'Not until…' He broke off. 'Not until I was sure you were going to be all right.'

She didn't want his sympathy. Hadn't she made that clear? Besides, he didn't have to worry about her anymore.

'He's mine,' she said. 'They're not going to take him from me.'

David looked over at her, his dark eyes warm with sympathy.

'I hope they don't take him,' he said. 'Anyone can see how much you love him.'

Olivia laughed shakily. 'No, they're really not going to take him. I heard a few minutes ago. The biological father has dropped the suit. Josh is going to stay with me.'

David's face broke into the grin she knew and loved so well. 'That's great news.' He reached for the hand that wasn't holding onto Josh. 'I couldn't be happier for you.'

'So you see, David, you don't have to concern yourself about me any more. I'm going to be just fine. Josh and I are going to be just fine.'

Back in New York, David tiptoed over to the hospital bed, but Lisa was awake. She smiled up at him and his heart contracted. Lisa had been admitted to hospital when her temperature had spiked.

She signalled with her eyes that she wanted her special keyboard, and when David placed it in front of her she began to type.

'Hey, big brother, what brings you here?'

'I heard you weren't doing so well,' he said. 'So I thought I should come and see for myself.'

'I'm doing okay,' she typed. 'But it's good to see you.'

'Where's Mom?' he asked.

'She's downstairs. Making phone calls. Some party she has to rearrange.'

David didn't know whether he was surprised. His mother would never change. Why he thought she would, he had no idea.

'I would have been here sooner, but Mom only called me last night to let me know you were in hospital.'

'Chest infection,' Lisa typed. 'Better now. You know how it is.'

Of course he knew. Lisa suffered from recurrent chest infections. Despite the fact his mother employed round-the-clock nurses, there was nothing anyone could do to keep the chest infections away all the time.

'What about work? How's that going?' Lisa typed.

'I'm planning to move back to New York,' David said. 'I've missed you.'

'And your girlfriend? The one who was pregnant? What about her?'

'She's doing okay. Her baby should be out of hospital soon. I think they'll manage fine.'

'And you? Will you manage fine without them?'

As always, David was surprised by his little sister's perspicacity. It made him feel ashamed all over again. He'd spent the first ten years after her accident running from his responsibilities. He'd told himself that it was because he couldn't bear seeing his kid sister struggle with even the smallest tasks, especially when that meant dealing with his mother on a daily basis, but the truth was every time he'd seen Lisa he'd felt guilty. He'd had the power to stop her taking off in the car. He'd known neither she nor her boyfriend had been fit to drive and while he'd tried to stop them, he hadn't tried hard enough.

'I think you need me more than they do,' he said. 'Mom clearly can't look after you properly.'

Lisa frowned. 'Mom looks after me the best she can. Don't want you to stay in New York. It will make me feel bad. Get on with your own life. That's what will make me happy.' She looked at him with her fierce green eyes and started typing again. 'Please, David. Don't muck up your own life because of me.'

'I'm not sure she even wants me,' he admitted.

'Not want you? Are you crazy? From what you've told me, she loves you. You're an idiot if you can't see that.'

Olivia loved him? He doubted that.

Just then his mother entered the room, still talking on the phone. She glanced at him. 'I've got to go,' she said to whoever she was speaking to. 'David's here.'

She replaced the phone in her bag and tipped her face up to receive David's kiss. 'That was your father on the phone,' she said to Lisa. 'Unfortunately he won't be able to come and see you, but he tells me to say hello.'

David tried not to wince. Couldn't his father, just this once, have made the effort to come and see his child? But David could count the number of times he'd visited his daughter on the fingers of one hand. Why should he expect him to have changed? Just because he himself had? Lisa and David exchanged a glance, and Lisa smiled. 'I don't mind,' she typed. 'Really.'

She should mind, David thought angrily. He minded for her.

'Perhaps Lisa should come and live with me,' he said to his mother, who was flicking through her diary.

'With you? I don't think that's appropriate, darling, do you? You'll be at work all day. Who will look after her?'

As if his mother wasn't out all day, leaving Lisa in the care of nurses, whom David knew were excellent but only paid to care for his sister after all.

'Thanks for the invite, David,' Lisa typed, 'but don't you think you should have asked me first? I don't want to move to San Francisco.'

'Lisa has met someone,' his mother piped up. She had seemed so engrossed in her diary he hadn't thought she was listening. 'She met him during one of her hospital check-ups and they've become quite close.'

Lisa's cheeks grew pink.

His baby sister was in love?

'Who is he?' David said. 'Because if he plays with you, he'll have me to answer to.'

Lisa flushed again. This time with anger. 'I'm thirty-five years old, David. Give me some credit.'

He did tend to forget his sister was a grown woman.

'Lisa has her own life, David,' his mother said mildly. 'And she makes sure she leads it. She always was a determined girl. If I try to interfere she tells me off. She can be quite insistent, you know.'

Had he been mistaken? Had he whisked in and out of the house so quickly that he hadn't noticed that it was all different? Lisa and his mother seemed to have an understanding that David had mistaken for lack of interest on his mother's part. Had he really been so angry with his mother that he'd never even considered the possibility she'd changed, and her apparently casual treatment of Lisa was born out of love and consideration for her younger daughter?

He looked more closely at his mother. The look in her eyes when she bent across to give Lisa a drink told him everything he needed to know. His father might be a write-off, his older sister too, and his brother too caught up with his own life to make more than rare appearances at home, but there was a bond between Lisa and his mother that seemed to be one of mutual love and respect. He'd been wrong about so many things, was it possible he'd been wrong about Olivia too? Had he finally, not before time, he had to admit, grown up sufficiently to know that if two people loved each other enough, they loved the whole of that person—warts and all?

But did Olivia love him? Had she seen past the facade he'd spent so long trying to perfect? Could she love the good, the bad and the ugly of him? He didn't know, but he knew he had to try.

CHAPTER SEVENTEEN

OLIVIA was exhausted. She'd been allowed to take Josh home after a couple of weeks and although she loved every moment of being with him, she had to admit that looking after a small baby was more tiring than she'd ever imagined.

She'd had loads of visitors. Everyone from the department had popped in at one time or another to admire little Josh and although it had been good to see them, it had made it difficult to establish a routine with her son

Dad had flown in for a week and had fallen instantly in love with Josh. But he'd been hurt and dismayed that Olivia had kept so much from him.

'You had no business keeping me in the dark,' he'd grumbled. 'I would have come if I'd known.'

'But you had Jennie to think about,' Olivia had replied. 'Don't you know how much I wanted you to have something of your own in your life?' She'd been sitting with her head on his lap, and he'd been stroking her hair. Josh for once was sleeping peacefully in his cot.

'Jennie would have understood. She has children of her own—and grandchildren. She knows more than most that when a child needs a parent, that parent comes running.'

'I'm sorry, Dad, I never meant to exclude you. It was

complicated.' She'd sighed. 'But everything's all right now. I have my baby. That's all I want.'

'Is it?' her father had said softly. 'Are you sure? What about this David you keep mentioning?'

'Do I?' Surely not.

'I can't tell you how often his name seems to come up, Olivia.' She'd heard the smile in her father's voice. 'Often enough for me to know that you love him.'

'Another bad choice, I'm afraid, Dad. David isn't the kind of man to take on a serious relationship, never mind another man's child.'

'Then he doesn't deserve you. You are worth more than that.'

'I only wish I didn't love him, Dad. He's not as bad as he thinks he is. He hasn't been brought up like I have— to know that while love can hurt, it can be worthwhile. I think he's frightened, that's all. One day, he'll meet the right woman. Someone who makes him realise the joy of loving more than makes up for the pain.'

In the end Olivia had practically to force her father onto the plane and back to New York. He and Jennie were due to marry in a couple of weeks, and Olivia knew her father missed his future wife terribly. The only reason he agreed to go was because she promised to come to the wedding and to bring Josh.

That had been last week. Her ticket and Josh's were booked to fly in a couple of days' time.

She peered into the cot. Josh was sleeping, his little arms waving every now and again as if he was dreaming. She would have a bath then, if he was awake, she would take him to the park in his pram. Bouncer needed a walk, and the fresh air might make her feel more alert.

Just then the doorbell rang and Bouncer woofed happily and ran to the door. More visitors, she thought.

Hopefully it would be someone who was happy to keep an eye on Josh while she had her bath.

But when she opened the door her heart felt as if it had stopped beating.

It was David.

Bouncer jumped up on David before doing an excited round of the sitting room. His excited barks woke Josh, who immediately started crying.

'Come in, David,' Olivia said, hurrying over to pick up her child. She wished she was wearing something other than an old shirt and faded jeans. She knew she looked bedraggled.

'Quiet, Bouncer,' David said sternly, and immediately Bouncer stopped his barking and sat down, only the rapid wagging of his tail revealing how excited he was. Perhaps when Josh was older she would take Bouncer to doggy school. He clearly could be taught.

'How are you, Olivia?' David asked. He walked over to her and peered down. 'Hello, Josh. You've grown since I saw you last.'

'What do you want, David?' Olivia asked. Why was he here? What did he want from her? Why couldn't he see that if he cared for her at all, she needed to be left to get on with her life?

'I wanted to see you.' David looked up from Josh. 'God, you look like…'

She laughed. Great. Just what she needed. Josh was still crying. He couldn't be hungry, he'd only just been fed before he'd gone down for his short nap, and as far as she could tell he was dry. But she should check. 'Look, let me turn the bath off and check Josh's nappy.'

'Why don't you carry on with your bath while I change him?' David suggested.

'You? With a nappy? Somehow I don't think so.'

But David had gently removed Josh from her arms. And to her amazement her son stopped crying instantly and gazed up at this new face with intense interest.

Even better. Now she looked a mess and clearly wasn't even able to look after her own child.

'Go for your bath, Olivia, I'll look after Josh. He'll be fine with me and Bouncer.' Bouncer wagged his tail in apparent agreement.

'I can't leave him with you. He's bound to start crying again.'

'I promise you, he'll be fine. I have held a baby before. In fact, I've got quite adept at settling Alice. Go on. Unless you want me to help you in?'

Olivia backed away hastily. The memory of the night he'd bathed her flooded back and she knew she was blushing furiously. She wouldn't put it past David to do exactly the same thing again.

And it was lovely, she thought as she sank beneath the suds a short time later. Lovely to know she could relax for ten minutes. Lovely to think she could close her eyes and not worry that she wouldn't hear Josh cry out for her. Lovely that David was here...whatever had brought him.

'Are you all right in there, Olivia?'

Olivia woke with a start. She'd been so tired she must have fallen asleep.

'Is Josh okay?'

'Sleeping like the baby he is.' There was a pause. 'Do you need a hand in there?' There was an undercurrent to his voice. Laughter—but something else she couldn't quite define.

'I'll be out in a minute,' she said hastily.

In fact, she was out in two. She dried herself quickly

and threw on the long cardigan she sometimes wore as a dressing gown. She wiped the haze from the mirror and peered into it. She did look like hell, but at least she'd washed her hair. It had had baby sick in it the last time she'd looked.

David, bouncing Josh in one arm, was stirring something in a pot from which there came a disturbing burning smell.

He glanced up at her with a frown. 'I thought I'd cook us some pasta with cheese sauce. I mean, how difficult could that be? But the damn thing has gone all lumpy.'

While she'd been in the bath he'd set the table—well, he'd laid the table with a couple of plates and some mismatched silverware—and lit a couple of candles. Olivia was bemused.

'Since we couldn't go out to dinner because of Josh, I thought I would make us something.' He picked up the saucepan and tipped the contents into a bin. 'Sorry. Looks like it's take-out after all.'

He looked so perplexed and disappointed that Olivia had to smile.

'David, why *are* you here?'

'Can we sit down?'

Olivia moved a pile of baby clothes from the couch and did as he asked. Josh had fallen asleep on David's shoulder. He was bound to wake in a few minutes, demanding to be fed.

David came to sit next to her. If she'd hoped that being apart from him would have dampened her feelings for him, or that her crush was all down to her hormones, she knew for certain that she'd been mistaken. David's energy filled the room, making the air vibrate.

'I've spent all my life trying to stay on the outside of other people's lives,' he said. 'At least, for as long as I can remember. I swore I would never get involved with anyone, at least not permanently.'

Olivia sighed. 'I know. We've been through this.'

'And the last person I ever wanted or imagined getting involved with was you.'

'You made that clear, too.'

'But every time I tried to distance myself I kept getting drawn back.'

'I know. And I'm sorry. I did appreciate you being around when I needed someone.' Good God, any more of this and she be tempted to hurl something at him. Couldn't he see that she knew? Knew only too well what a trial she had been?

'But now I can't imagine life without you. Nothing seems right any more. All I can think of is you. What you are doing. Is your hair falling over your face? Are you laughing with someone else? Damn it, Olivia, it's driving me crazy.'

Her heart was doing a crazy little dance somewhere deep inside. Nevertheless, if he had something to say he needed to spell it out.

'I love you, can't you see that?'

He sounded angry, not loving at all.

She waited with her hands folded on her lap.

'Don't you have anything to say?' David demanded.

'I'm not sure what you want me to say. From what I can gather, you're telling me that you love me, but you don't want to be involved with me. Have I got it right?'

She hid another smile at the look of incredulity on his face. Well, if David Stuart wanted her to fall down in gratitude because he loved her but didn't want to be with her, he had another think coming. However, a warm, happy feeling was spreading from deep in her chest down to her toes. He loved her. And she believed him—

well, almost. Could you really stay away from someone you loved and who loved you back? She couldn't. A chill ran up her spine. Maybe this was the line David took with all his women. A kind of bizarre, letting-down-gently approach. Her head was beginning to ache. Maybe it was lack of sleep but she still couldn't make head or tail of why he was here.

She noticed that Josh had left a line of sick down David's cashmere sweater. She leaned over and gently removed her son and placed him in his cot.

When she returned, David was pacing up and down. He swung round.

'You're not making this easy for me, woman.'

Suddenly she was furious. She didn't know what game David was playing but she wanted no part of it.

'Let me get this right. Over the last few months you've waltzed in and out of my life—oh…' she held up a hand as he started to protest '…I know you've been helping me and I appreciate that, but you make love to me, make me think you feel something for me and then—nothing. Later, you appear again, this time to tell me you're planning to return to New York. Fine. I didn't try to stop you. Then…' She was aware that she had balled her hands into fists. 'Then I hear via Kelly that you've decided not to take the job in New York after all and then more nothing. Silence. Fine. Now you knock on my door, asking me to go to dinner as if that's perfectly reasonable after weeks of silence—and after that you go on about loving me but not wanting to be involved. Forgive me, David, if I'm being a little obtuse here. I love you, but what the hell are you up to?'

She was breathing heavily, but instead of seeming chastened by her outburst David was grinning.

'And if you dare say something like "God, you look beautiful when you're angry", so help me...'

'I may be twice your size but it won't stop you throwing me out the door.' His grin grew wider. 'Now, why don't I find that difficult to believe?' His smile vanished and he narrowed his eyes.

'Whoa, back up. Did you just say you love me?'

'Of course I love you. You must know that. You can't be that stupid.'

He stepped towards her and took her face in his large hands. 'Say it again.'

Olivia was almost crying with fury and frustration. She shook her head. 'No. You've had everything out of me that I can give you. I can't pretend I don't love you, not even to save my pride, but you'll get nothing more from me. Please. Just go.'

Gently he rubbed the pads of his thumbs under her eyes.

'And that's a reason to cry?' he said hoarsely.

Olivia hadn't even known she was crying. She looked up at him.

He brought his mouth down on hers and his kiss was everything she remembered and more.

When he let her go she was shaking.

'I've never proposed to anyone before. Can you blame me for making a pig's ear of it?'

'You're proposing?'

'I love you. I can't imagine my life without you. Didn't I say that? I want to spend every day with you and every night. I want us to have children together. I want to have everything with you. For God's sake, say you'll marry me.'

'And Josh? What about him?'

'He's part of you. A cute part of you—if a messy one.

I'll do my best to be a father to him. If you'll let me?
You'll have to teach me, Olivia, you'll have to help me
be a better man than I am, but...' His fingertips trailed
down the side of her neck and a shock of desire coursed
through her body. 'I'll practise every day.' He kissed her
nose. Just like I'll practise this...' he moved to her col-
larbone '...and this.'

'I think you're a good man already,' she said, inhaling the scent of him. 'But why don't you kiss me again?
And see if you can convince me?'

* * * * *

Mills & Boon® Hardback

September 2012

ROMANCE

Unlocking her Innocence	Lynne Graham
Santiago's Command	Kim Lawrence
His Reputation Precedes Him	Carole Mortimer
The Price of Retribution	Sara Craven
Just One Last Night	Helen Brooks
The Greek's Acquisition	Chantelle Shaw
The Husband She Never Knew	Kate Hewitt
When Only Diamonds Will Do	Lindsay Armstrong
The Couple Behind the Headlines	Lucy King
The Best Mistake of Her Life	Aimee Carson
The Valtieri Baby	Caroline Anderson
Slow Dance with the Sheriff	Nikki Logan
Bella's Impossible Boss	Michelle Douglas
The Tycoon's Secret Daughter	Susan Meier
She's So Over Him	Joss Wood
Return of the Last McKenna	Shirley Jump
Once a Playboy...	Kate Hardy
Challenging the Nurse's Rules	Janice Lynn

MEDICAL

Her Motherhood Wish	Anne Fraser
A Bond Between Strangers	Scarlet Wilson
The Sheikh and the Surrogate Mum	Meredith Webber
Tamed by her Brooding Boss	Joanna Neil

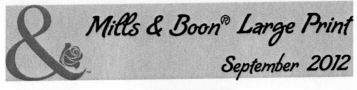

Mills & Boon® Large Print

September 2012

ROMANCE

A Vow of Obligation	Lynne Graham
Defying Drakon	Carole Mortimer
Playing the Greek's Game	Sharon Kendrick
One Night in Paradise	Maisey Yates
Valtieri's Bride	Caroline Anderson
The Nanny Who Kissed Her Boss	Barbara McMahon
Falling for Mr Mysterious	Barbara Hannay
The Last Woman He'd Ever Date	Liz Fielding
His Majesty's Mistake	Jane Porter
Duty and the Beast	Trish Morey
The Darkest of Secrets	Kate Hewitt

HISTORICAL

Lady Priscilla's Shameful Secret	Christine Merrill
Rake with a Frozen Heart	Marguerite Kaye
Miss Cameron's Fall from Grace	Helen Dickson
Society's Most Scandalous Rake	Isabelle Goddard
The Taming of the Rogue	Amanda McCabe

MEDICAL

Falling for the Sheikh She Shouldn't	Fiona McArthur
Dr Cinderella's Midnight Fling	Kate Hardy
Brought Together by Baby	Margaret McDonagh
One Month to Become a Mum	Louisa George
Sydney Harbour Hospital: Luca's Bad Girl	Amy Andrews
The Firebrand Who Unlocked His Heart	Anne Fraser

Mills & Boon® Hardback

October 2012

ROMANCE

Banished to the Harem	Carol Marinelli
Not Just the Greek's Wife	Lucy Monroe
A Delicious Deception	Elizabeth Power
Painted the Other Woman	Julia James
A Game of Vows	Maisey Yates
A Devil in Disguise	Caitlin Crews
Revelations of the Night Before	Lynn Raye Harris
Defying her Desert Duty	Annie West
The Wedding Must Go On	Robyn Grady
The Devil and the Deep	Amy Andrews
Taming the Brooding Cattleman	Marion Lennox
The Rancher's Unexpected Family	Myrna Mackenzie
Single Dad's Holiday Wedding	Patricia Thayer
Nanny for the Millionaire's Twins	Susan Meier
Truth-Or-Date.com	Nina Harrington
Wedding Date with Mr Wrong	Nicola Marsh
The Family Who Made Him Whole	Jennifer Taylor
The Doctor Meets Her Match	Annie Claydon

MEDICAL

A Socialite's Christmas Wish	Lucy Clark
Redeeming Dr Riccardi	Leah Martyn
The Doctor's Lost-and-Found Heart	Dianne Drake
The Man Who Wouldn't Marry	Tina Beckett

Mills & Boon® Large Print

October 2012

ROMANCE

A Secret Disgrace — Penny Jordan
The Dark Side of Desire — Julia James
The Forbidden Ferrara — Sarah Morgan
The Truth Behind his Touch — Cathy Williams
Plain Jane in the Spotlight — Lucy Gordon
Battle for the Soldier's Heart — Cara Colter
The Navy SEAL's Bride — Soraya Lane
My Greek Island Fling — Nina Harrington
Enemies at the Altar — Melanie Milburne
In the Italian's Sights — Helen Brooks
In Defiance of Duty — Caitlin Crews

HISTORICAL

The Duchess Hunt — Elizabeth Beacon
Marriage of Mercy — Carla Kelly
Unbuttoning Miss Hardwick — Deb Marlowe
Chained to the Barbarian — Carol Townend
My Fair Concubine — Jeannie Lin

MEDICAL

Georgie's Big Greek Wedding? — Emily Forbes
The Nurse's Not-So-Secret Scandal — Wendy S. Marcus
Dr Right All Along — Joanna Neil
Summer With A French Surgeon — Margaret Barker
Sydney Harbour Hospital: Tom's Redemption — Fiona Lowe
Doctor on Her Doorstep — Annie Claydon